ANOTHER D FOR DEEDEE

ANOTHER D FOR DEEDEE

BIBI BELFORD

Sky Pony Press
New York

Sky Pony Press books may be purchased in bulk at special discounts for sales promotion, corporate gifts, fund-raising, or educational purposes. Special editions can also be created to specifications. For details, contact the Special Sales Department, Sky Pony Press, 307 West 36th Street, 11th Floor, New York, NY 10018 or info@skyhorsepublishing.com.

Sky Pony® is a registered trademark of Skyhorse Publishing, Inc.®, a Delaware corporation.

Visit our website at www.skyponypress.com.

www.BibiBelford.com

10 9 8 7 6 5 4 3 2

Library of Congress Cataloging-in-Publication Data is available on file.

Cover design by Sammy Yuen
Cover photographs: iStockphoto

Paperback ISBN: 978-1-5107-2406-8
Ebook ISBN: 978-1-5107-2407-5

Printed in the United States of America

This book is dedicated to Dreamers everywhere.
Those who dream to belong.
Those who dream to be accepted.
And those who make dreams come true.

CHAPTER ONE

D IS FOR DARE

"Come on, DeeDee. Choose already. Truth or dare?" says my bossy big sister Danita with her Passion-Pink-lip-gloss lips. Hope you don't have one. A bossy sister, I mean, not a Passion Pink lip gloss.

"I'm thinking, I'm thinking," I say. And I am. I'm thinking I hate this game. Danita loves it. So does Andrea, my sister's new friend, maybe even her new best friend. "Okay, truth."

"So, which boy would you pick to k—" Andrea starts.

"No, I changed my mind. I meant DARE," I scream in her face.

1

"Oh-Em-Gee DeeDee, that's not how you play. You can't change your mind."

"Give me the dare."

"Okay. We dare you to swallow the drink of death." Danita goes to the kitchen, and I hear a spoon clinking around in a glass.

"What is it?" I ask when she gives me the drink. I smell coffee and something else—vinegar, maybe. Or pickle juice. It's very muddy looking.

Danita whispers something in Andrea's ear and they giggle. They think their you-know-whats don't stink, just because they're in eighth grade.

Danita's so lucky. She met Andrea last week, on the day we moved into our new apartment. And it just so happens that Andrea goes to Joyner Middle School, where Danita will be starting tomorrow. Joyner sounds nice, doesn't it? Like a place to join right in. I'm in fourth grade. And I'm starting at Robert Frost. Now, how does that sound? Robert Frost? Brrrr. Chilly. Especially since I don't know one single person at my new school.

I hate being the little sister. I pinch my nose and take a sip of the drink of death. The powdered coffee isn't even dissolved. Gross. And something gooey is sticking the coffee specks to my tongue so I can't swallow them. I may barf. But Danita and Andrea are laughing at the face I'm making. I chug the rest down, stick out my tongue with the coffee grounds on it, and yell all the way to the bathroom to rinse my mouth. I stop up the drain and fill the sink so I can stick my face all the way in.

"Gordita." Mami is at the door. "Gordita. Too much noise. Time for bed."

"You're home!" I rush over to hug her. She smells delicious. Like pizza. Guess why? She makes the dough at Papa Giapino's Pizza. And since Papi went to Mexico to take care of his sick grandmother, my bisabuelita, Danita babysits me when Mami works late. Like I'm a baby or something.

"The water, Gordita, the water."

Whoops, the sink is overflowing. I turn off the water and sop it up off the floor.

"I bring pizza for you. Eat fast."

When I get to the living room, I see only three pieces of pizza, and a half liter of soda.

"Oh My Gatos, you pigs." I shove myself in between Danita and Andrea and grab the three pieces. I don't mean to knock the box on the floor. It just happens.

"Mami, tell her to stop!" yells Danita.

"The box was half empty to start," Andrea tells me.

"You dork." Danita jabs me with her bony elbow, making me spill the soda I'm guzzling. "You better learn some manners. You don't have much time before my *quinceañera*."

I spray a little soda from my mouth in Danita's direction. "Your birthday isn't till May and it's only January. Nobody wants to go to your stupid *quinceañera*, anyway!"

Danita pinches me and Andrea holds in a laugh.

"Dinora, *te portas bien*," Mami says from the door.

Dinora is my real name, By The Way. Which I hate, By The Way. And why is she telling me to behave? What about Danita?

Mami's in her fuzzy robe already.

"I speak English. ENGLISH!" I have not spoken one word of Spanish since Thanksgiving when Papi didn't come back from Mexico like Mami said he would. Not one word. I do not believe Papi went to Mexico to take care of my *bisabuelita*. Not anymore. Nobody goes to Mexico and forgets to come home for Thanksgiving. NOBODY. Everybody from our old trailer park knew we were at the shelter. EVERYBODY. And if Papi did come home after we moved SOMEBODY would tell him. But now? Now that Mami made us move to this apartment? Now, I don't know. And I do not answer to Dinora. BY THE WAY.

I get ready for bed. Still mad. And still thirsty. With the awful taste of coffee in my mouth. Gross. I drank that soda so fast that I keep burping the coffee taste up. Double gross.

To tell the truth, I get ready for couch and not bed. Our trailer park caught on fire the week before winter break. The Red Cross helped us relocate to this apartment and get new stuff. My old school gave us lots of presents and donations. We're still unpacking.

But since this apartment only has three bedrooms, my options are:

1) Air mattress on the floor in Danita's or Danny's room. Can you say creepy crawlies?
2) My mami's double bed. Can you say stinky breath?
3) The comfy couch. Really, the best option, don't you think?

Mami shoos Danita and Andrea out of the living room and tucks the sheets around the couch for me. She always puts a plastic tablecloth over the cushions. I don't know why. Well, actually, I do. Sometimes I have a little accident. But you don't have to go blabbing about it.

I take my shower because I take a shower every night and I admire my new princess pj's in the steamy mirror. I suck in my belly. I feel skinnier. I really do. Maybe they're secretly slimming pj's. They're very slippery as I slide under my fluffy-fleecy blanket, the one that my godmother in Mexico sent me and that Danita wrapped me up in the night of the fire. The plastic tablecloth makes wrapping-paper sounds. Mami kisses me.

I got the pj's from my old school's Secret Swap for the holidays. Instead of everybody swapping gifts with each other, they gave me all the gifts because all my stuff got burned up. And like I said before, other people, parents and teachers, donated bunches of stuff.

I'm not complaining, but some of the things they donated are not exactly my style.

Danita says, "Beggars can't be choosers."

Mami says, "Blessings come from Heaven."

I say, "Let the beggars choose the blessings."

Anyway, the pajamas are nice—a little babyish with lots of sparkle and glitter. Of course, I would never wear them to a sleepover. Not that I'm likely to get invited to a sleepover, and even if I did, there's my little accident problem anyway.

I hear my brother Daniel come in, turn the deadbolt, and go to the kitchen. I see the side of his face as he stands in front of the fridge, hunting for food. He doesn't look like my brother Danny anymore, the one with the laughing eyes, the color of my Burnished Brown crayon. I have to memorize this new Daniel. The new tattoo—two curlicued Ds, separated by a feathery arrow. The long arms that reach almost to his knees. The new man-voice when he talks.

He forgets to turn out the kitchen light and walks into the living room, eating. He stands behind my couch. I hear him breathing.

"What are you doing, Danny?"

"*¡Ay!* You scared me. Why aren't you sleeping? Did I wake you up?"

"Nope. Me and Osito are wide awake." I hold up my teddy. My teddy bear from when I was a little baby, which Mami miraculously rescued from our trailer.

I pull my legs up and Danny sits down. I tuck my cold toes under him. In the shadowy light his face reminds me of Papi.

I can't think of one thing to say to my brother. Danny's been gone for twenty-seven weeks. I know. I counted. It was the beginning of summer and the end of third grade when he left. And he's been home for four weeks. I know. I counted. Christmas Eve. That's when Danny came walking into the shelter with a big garbage bag full of presents. Even his National Guard training program heard about our trailer and gave us presents. And Mami got all slobbery. In public. Super embarrassing. We all knew Danny was supposed to come home after twenty weeks, like most of the other boys, but we didn't ask him about it. Maybe it took him longer to be trained. Or maybe he didn't want to live in the shelter with us.

I want to ask Danny to tell me the story of why he dropped out of Northlake High School even though Papi told him not to. And to tell me if it was fun being in the National Guard for dropouts. And if the Danny I used to know—the funny one who belched in my face—will be back someday.

"How's night school?" It's the only thing I dare to ask.

"All right, I guess. Pretty boring. Everything is on the computer. You start back tomorrow?"

"Yep. Another new school. Robert Frost." That makes four since I started kindergarten. Washington, Jefferson, Lincoln, and now Frost.

"The poet."

"What?"

"Robert Frost was a poet."

"Oh." So, three president schools and one poet school.

"Think they'll name a school after you someday?" I wiggle my toes to tickle him.

"Ever hear of Dropout Elementary?" Danny says. "They don't name schools after dropouts."

"You're not a dropout anymore. And didn't Papi used to say everyone makes mistakes? Maybe even Robert Frost."

Danny folds his arms and puts his chin on his chest. He lets out a sigh. "How about Dinora Diaz School?"

"Never." I kick him. Not hard. He knows I hate Dinora. For three reasons:

1) No one can pronounce it. They say Die-Nora. Or Die-No-Ray. Or Dine-Ora.

2) When you pronounce it Dine-Ora, my name sounds like dinosaur. And nobody wants to be called Dinosaur.

3) Even if you pronounce it correctly, Dee-Nor-Ah, nobody is named Dinora, not one single

soul. No singers. No dancers. No presidents. And no poets. Who wants to be friends with a girl named Dinora? It's a stupid-dopey name.

"How about Gordita Grammar School?" Danny says.

This time I kick him hard. Only Mami and Papi are allowed to call me Gordita. They've called me that ever since I was a fat baby. I'm just a little fat now. Pudgy. But not skinny. Not like Flaquita-Danita and her stupid-dopey friend. Who wants to be that skinny?

"Don't worry." Danny grabs my toes. "You'll make lots of friends. As long as you don't kick them."

"Maybe a best friend." I snuggle my face into my blanket and cross my fingers. On both hands. But I don't get my hopes up. It seems as though everybody already has a BFF by the time I transfer to a new school.

"There's a kid your age I think, right next door," Danny says.

"Really?" I raise my head. "What's her name?"

"How should I know? You'll have to find out. Maybe you can walk to school together."

Papi always says that to me when I ask him stuff. How should I know, DeeDee? You'll have to find out.

"Is Papi ever coming home?" I only dare whisper this question. If Danny doesn't hear me, then he won't have to answer.

Danny stiffens. He cracks his knuckles. "How should I know, DeeDee?" His voice is soft, raspy, like he's swallowed too many hot peppers.

We all think maybe Papi went to live in Mexico. He always talked about going back there. Over and over. Like those annoying commercials on TV.

Danny moves his fingers around the tattoo swirls on his wrist. Tracing each D and then the arrow.

"What if he doesn't want to come back? What if he likes it in Mexico?" I pull Danny's arm to me and run my fingers over the tattoo. "DeeDee," I say. I know it stands for Daniel Diaz, but I like to pretend. I will never get a tattoo. I'm afraid of needles. Really afraid.

"You know more than me about Papi leaving. You were here," Danny says.

"He wanted you to come home and for all of us to move to Mexico. He told Mami you needed a start-over," I say.

"You mean a do-over, a fresh start. You don't even understand Papi's Spanish."

"Yes I do. He said start-over."

Danny pulls his arm from me and rubs his neck. "Fine. Then what?"

"Danita told him moving to Mexico would ruin her life and she would hate him forever."

"What did Mami say?" asks Danny.

"Mami said she would never come back if they moved to Mexico." I'm not positive about this. She might have said she could never come back. I don't know for sure, because Danny's right—sometimes I do get mixed up when the meaning is close in Spanish.

I remember the day of the argument. Papi's face. So sad. Mami's face. So scared.

"And anyway," I tell Danny, "Mami told him we didn't have passports or money to get them."

I don't tell Danny what I said. Because maybe that's the real reason Papi left. His little Gordita, taking sides with Mami and Danita. All you care about is yourself. That's what I said. Because I was worried about missing the Secret Swap at school. Because I thought maybe, for once, somebody would want to be my best friend. I mean who wouldn't want to be best friends with me, the giver of a super cool up-cycled bike, the awesomest Secret Swap gift ever?

Danny stays quiet for a minute and I'm afraid he's going to ask me what I said to Papi. Then he says, "I don't know, DeeDee. I don't know. Let me worry about it, okay? It's a grown-up problem."

I wonder if Papi said goodbye to Danny before he left. I bet he didn't. He didn't say goodbye to me or Danita. I tuck my teddy bear under my blanket. "Danita says maybe he got fired from his job and now her *quinceañera* will be canceled."

"Because she knows everything, doesn't she? Like her *quinceañera* is the most important thing in the world." Danny makes a grunting noise. "And anyway, if Mami wants to give her a *quinceañera*, she will do it no matter what. Stop worrying about it, okay? I'm going to shower."

"Wait, can I go pee before you go in there?"

Before I zip out of the bathroom, I take big gulps of water right from the faucet. That pizza made me so thirsty. When I come back, Danny tucks the blanket around my toes. "Night, DeeDee."

I hear noises. The bark of a dog. The slam of a door. The siren of an ambulance. I can't get to sleep. I guess I'm nervous about going to school. Explaining to another teacher that my name is DeeDee and not Dinora. Hoping I don't have to make a stink about it. Hoping somebody will sit by me at lunch. Hoping that maybe—well, I'm not going to say it. If I say it, it might not ever come true.

And I'm thinking about Papi. I know the real reason he's gone. Danita doesn't know. And neither does Danny. I know.

Papi deserted us. He left his dropout son and his disagreeable daughter. He left his disappointing Gordita and his stubborn wife who only speaks Spanish. And that's the truth. It makes me sad. And mad, too. How dare you? I want to say to him. How dare you?

CHAPTER TWO

D IS FOR D (DUH)

Danita stands in front of the hall mirror. First front-ways. Then sideways. "I am so fat," she says, grabbing at her waist.

I pull on leggings and a pink top with a ruffle. I twirl like a ballerina so it spins out.

"Danita, *no te preocupes por tus masitas*," I hear Mami say.

Love handles? Those tiny ripples are her love handles? Well, if Danita's not supposed to worry about her love handles, then my belly must be the entire love pot. I take off the leggings and the ruffly shirt, squeeze into my last pair of clean jeans, and yank one of my two sparkly T-shirts over my head—the purple one. It feels like a purple day, not a pink one.

I rush to eat breakfast and Mami rushes to answer the knock on the door. It's Andrea, in her skinny leg dark wash jeans, leather boots with sheep fur sticking out, and a puffy silver jacket. She has about a million braids that dance around her head.

"Ooh, what a sparkly shirt," she says to me. "All ready for your first day?"

Danita comes in and grabs her jacket. She's wearing eye makeup. Papi never let her wear makeup. "Mami," I start to tattle, and Danita narrows her eyes at me.

Andrea says, "Your little sister looks just like you."

Danita opens the door and before I can finish tattling, says, "I was never that pudgy," and slams the door shut.

Mami has to walk me to school to deliver my school folder to the office. Like I'm such a baby I can't handle a simple folder. I keep my eyes straight ahead, walking one sidewalk square in front of Mami, so nobody notices she's with me. She could be anybody's mother, or some lady taking a walk. While she waits for help at the office counter I get a long drink at the water fountain. Then I stand at the back of the office, watching the students streaming into school.

Everything seems different here. Not like Lincoln Elementary.

1) Colder drinking fountains.

2) No translator for Mami.

3) Fancy jeans and UGG boots on every other girl.

Mami hands me a slip of paper with a room number, #131, and a name, MRS. KREWELL. "*Te portas bien*, Dinora," says Mami and starts to kiss me. I do not like kissing. By The Way. And I do not answer to Dinora. Just a reminder. I'm in the hallway in two seconds before anybody sees me with that lady who just happens to be my mother.

And something else is different here. At Lincoln Elementary the office people take new kids on a tour. And they make an announcement after the morning pledge. "Today we'd like to welcome Blah Blah to fourth grade. Please show Blah Blah that Together We Make a Difference. Remember Lincoln students. Be safe. Be kind. Be smart."

Well, maybe Robert Frost was going to give me a tour, but I ran out of the office too fast. And now I'm totally lost. I turn corners and corners and the numbers above the doors make no sense. If somebody asks me to build a school, I'm going to make one long giant hallway with numbers 1 to 131 all in a row. I feel like Anna running lost, looking for Elsa's frozen castle in an unfriendly winter. No one helps me. No one talks to me. No one looks like me.

Well, finally. Here's #13_. I guess the one fell off and no one told me. The tardy bell rings just as I open the door. I keep my backpack on, stand at the door, and wait. I wish I had a desk to hide in. I watch as the teacher, a tall woman with puffy hair and large hoop earrings highlights the parts of a poem on the interactive white board. I don't know how to pronounce her name from the slip of paper. I do know that at Lincoln Elementary, Miss Hamilton would still be taking attendance.

"Line. Stanza. Meter. Beat. Rhyme scheme." The students use iPads to follow along. Everyone has an iPad? We only had six at Lincoln and we shared them with another class.

Finally, the teacher notices me. She walks to the door with a sour-apple face.

"The office didn't tell me I was getting a new student." She touches a button on the wall.

My hands start to sweat.

"Front office," says a voice from the speaker above the button.

I rub my palms on my too-tight jeans.

"I didn't get any notification that I was getting a new student," says Sour-Apple Face.

"I'm sorry. Her mother brought the files instead of sending them ahead," says the voice.

I pull my shirt down and my backpack rises up behind my head.

"I think I have more students than the other fourth grades," says Sourpuss.

"Just a minute, let me check," says the voice.

My neck itches and I sneak a peek at the class. A girl with black, arrow-straight hair whispers to a girl in a pink fuzzy vest and they giggle. Other girls lean in, as though the dark-haired girl is a vacuum. Jazzy, one of my almost-friends from Lincoln, was like that, too. But in a good way. Like a magnet. Or like the sun. I sure don't feel like a magnet or the sun standing in the door. And I wish a real vacuum would come along and get me out of here.

"Mrs. Krewell," says the voice. Did she say Cruella? Well, that seems about right.

"Yes," says Mrs. Cruella. The kind of yes where your voice goes up at the end, to show the other person how limited your patience is.

"You're correct, you do have higher numbers." Well, Good Gatos. I'm glad I don't have to be in this sourpuss's room. I turn to leave. "But your new student belongs in the cluster for interventions, so she's been placed in your room."

Mrs. Cruella raises her eyebrows. "Well, then I will need a desk," she says to the voice coming from the wall.

She points to the table at the back of the room. "You can sit there—what did you say your name was?—until they bring you a desk."

"DeeDee," I say. "DeeDee Diaz." At least I didn't have to explain about my name being DeeDee and not Dinora.

I head to the table and take off my backpack. I'm used to waiting for a desk. Kids stare. Well, I'm used to that, too. Mrs. Cruella gets back to teaching.

The door opens. It's a girl with thick hair like mine and tan skin. A Latina girl. The first one I've seen.

"Tell Mr. Somerset we're using our iPads this morning," says Mrs. Cruella.

My desk arrives. Along with my records folder. And Mrs. Cruella motions me to move. I scramble to dump a few things into my desk.

Heads bend down to finish work, but I know eyes are still stealing peeks at me. Mrs. Cruella walks around the room, checking iPads and correcting some students' work. Then she rips off large sheets of paper from a hanging pad.

She holds up a hand. "Give me five, everyone."

I look around. Five what? The girl behind me points to a poster on the wall. GIVE ME FIVE. Eyes watch. Ears listen. Lips closed. Hands empty. Body still.

Once everyone settles down, Mrs. Cruella says, "Okay class. Get started on your group projects. DeeDee, work with Nancy's group."

I look around. Guess who Nancy is—straight-arrow hair girl. Vacuum girl. Of course. Three more girls come toward my desk. I'm not sure what to do.

"Put your backpack in the hallway," Nancy says to me, putting the chart paper on my desk. "It's in the way."

Before I can stop the words, they've escaped from my mouth. "Why don't you mind your own business?" It's as if I sprayed Raid on a bunch of cockroaches. Complete silence. Everyone in the group gawks at me. Nancy doesn't move. Then, she picks up my backpack and hands it to me. Without a word, I walk to the hall and hang it on a hook with no name above it. I dig down to the bottom of the outside pouch and find a little bag of M&M's. I open it and pour all of them into my mouth. I chew while I scan some of the names above the hooks.

Chloe Anderson, Arianna Brown, Andrew Johnson, Nicole Swanson, Nancy Wang . . .

Where are the Martinez, Garcia, and Hernandez names? Not in my class, apparently. Not like at Lincoln Elementary, where more than half my class spoke Spanish.

When I get back to the group, they're discussing what our poem should be about. Nancy makes a sniffing noise when I sit down. "Chocolate," she whispers and glares at me.

Each time someone makes a suggestion, Nancy makes a comment. "I think that's too complicated, Samantha." and then Samantha says, "Oh it is, isn't it?" Or Nancy says, "Hmmm. I don't know Nicole," and then Nicole says, "Yah. I don't know either."

I wish I could go back in time. Back to before Christmas. Before my trailer burned down. Back to Lincoln

and the Secret Swap, when Jazzy gave me a skateboard—an awesome decked out skateboard. Maybe,
if we didn't move, we'd be best friends. Then I get an
idea.

"What if we write a poem about going back in
time?" I ask.

"That's a good idea," says Nicole. "I wish I could
go back in time . . ."

"Before I had to make this rhyme," I say.

"Do the next one, Samantha," says Nicole.

A blonde girl with the bluest eyes says, "Before
stanza, meter, beat, and line."

The girl who giggled with Nancy when I first came
into the room says, "Back in time would be so fine."

We all clap and Samantha says, "That's perfect,
Sherie."

All except Nancy. She purses her lips. "No. It will
be too hard to illustrate. What would we draw? I think
we should do cats."

And that's that. Cats. But I don't have to help, do I?
So I sit there. Until Mrs. Cruella asks Nancy if everyone is participating in the group.

"Oh yes," she says. "DeeDee is doing the illustra-
tions."

And I do. I make the ugliest cat you've ever seen.
To go with the ugliest poem you've ever heard.

"You've ruined it," hisses Nancy.

I shrug. Oh well.

Then it's time for math.

•

"DeeDee. DeeDee."

"Yes. Yes. Can't you see me? I'm here, under the sea on the trampoline filled with jellyfish."

"DeeDee."

The jellyfish are tapping me, pushing me, shaking me. It's so wet here under the water.

"DeeDee."

My eyes snap open. I freeze. Solid freeze. An ice-cube-in-January freeze. Oh My Gatos. I'm not under the sea. There's no more jellyfish. Just me at my desk with a very sick feeling in my stomach and a wet seat. And bunches of kids I don't even know staring at me.

"You fell asleep, DeeDee. Do you feel all right?" Mrs. Cruella stands next to my desk. I grab my jacket from the back of my chair and put it over my lap, letting the sleeves hang down to cover the puddle that's dripping to the floor.

I feel like saying, *No, duh. I don't feel all right. I feel tired. And wet. And over this school.*

But instead I say, "I guess I stayed up too late watching *Scream if You're Scared.*" And I laugh in an evil voice, pulling my jacket around my legs. It's not true. Mami would never let me watch that. But nobody needs to feel sorry for me, especially not Mrs. Cruella, or Nancy. Noodlenose Nancy, I decide to call her.

Mrs. Cruella frowns at me, but I see Samantha and Nicole smile, impressed, and I manage to stay awake the rest of the morning. At lunch, I wait until everyone leaves the classroom. Mrs. Cruella pokes her head back in the door to check on me while I'm busily finishing math problems.

"Hurry up, DeeDee. We'll wait for you in the hall."

My heart is hammering. Oh Land O'Lakes. No one saw. Did they? This has never happened at school before. And I do not cry about things. I do not.

When she closes the door I put my assignment on her desk, run to get paper towels, sop up my chair and my pants, and tie my jacket around my waist. I notice someone left their hoodie lying on their desk. I'm not sure when we'll do laundry at home and I don't have any other jackets, so to be on the safe side, I grab it, run to the hall, stuff it in my backpack, and get in line.

All during recess, while I'm sitting on the cold floor watching a movie, I think about Lincoln and my friends. Well, my almost-friends. Things were so much better there. Nobody had all these fancy clothes or whole class iPads. I was popular there. Well, kind of popular. At least a few people liked me. I think. I guess I did get into some trouble. And Jazzy accused me of stealing her favorite crayon, but I was going to put it back. And

I was on check-in, check-out for my homework and behavior. But I was starting to change. I really was.

No one talks to me at recess or lunch. Nancy seems to be in charge of the table and she and Sherie are too busy talking to notice me help myself to a bag of chips left in the middle of the table. But when I ask to use the bathroom, I hear a giggle. I gulp. Does someone know I wet my pants? I swipe a second cookie from the lunch cart on my way to the bathroom.

I lean on the wall across from the bathroom and read the posters. BOOK FAIR. BOGO. BUY ONE, GET ONE FREE. I make a new discovery. The letters of BUY ONE, GET ONE FREE make the word BOGO. I guess I never took the time to figure that out before. Maybe I'll make up my own language. LMA—Leave me alone. WNFA—Who needs friends anyway?

Another poster announces ANNUAL ROBERT FROST SPRING FLING. THE THING TO SHOW YOUR BLING ON THE FIRST DAY OF SPRING. JUDGED BY SLT. I try to puzzle that one out. Salt? Silt? Slit? And one more I can't say out loud.

"Are you going to try out?"

I turn to see Samantha.

"Are you kidding? Show your bling?" I say and roll my eyes.

"It's actually pretty fun," she says. "Nancy always dances. But you can do anything, even create your own category. As long as the Student Leadership Team votes for you."

Ah. SLT—Student Leadership Team.

"Anything?" I ask. "Even drawing ugly cats?"

Samantha laughs, and the bathroom door opens. I scoot in quickly, my jacket hanging way down around my waist.

I consider going to the nurse after lunch, because I'm uncomfortable in my wet pants, and I still feel tired, so maybe I am getting sick, but then what? Nobody will rescue me. Mami and Danny both work in the afternoon. Mami either at Giapino's or her cleaning job, and Danny at Walt's Finer Foods. I can stick it out and take a nap when I get home. I raise my hand to get a drink. Maybe that will wake me up. Mrs. Cruella nods. When I get back she motions me to the table in the back of the room.

"I'm sorry we got started on the wrong foot, DeeDee. I've been going over your records from Lincoln Elementary during lunch. It looks like you have a hard time in reading. Do you know what your reading grade has been for the past two years?" She taps a shiny silver mechanical pencil on my record sheet.

I wait, but she doesn't go on so I guess she wants me to answer.

"I've moved around a lot and maybe I got behind." From the corner of my eye I see Nancy eavesdropping.

"So you know what your reading grade is?"

"D?" I whisper.

"That's right. And D means needs improvement."

Duh, I almost say out loud. And D means Dumb.

"Do you speak Spanish? Sometimes reading can be more difficult while you're learning English."

"No." I say in a louder voice. "No, I do not." A lot of nerve she has. Just because my name is Dinora Diaz doesn't mean I speak Spanish. Of course, I do speak Spanish. And Papi wants me to speak better Spanish. Well, a lot of nerve he has too.

"My job is to make you successful, but I'll need your help. For starters, will you try to get to bed on time?" she asks and in a whisper adds, "So you don't have any more accidents?"

I keep my eyes down and my mouth closed. How did she know?

"And I'm going to sign you up for a peer tutor. I think that will really help get you back on track." Mrs. Cruella gets up from the little table and digs around in her desk drawer. While she's gone, I calmly put her shiny mechanical pencil in the waistband of my shorts.

When she comes back, she slides a paper in front of me. "This explains peer tutoring. One of my former students, Yari, might be available. You two will really get along."

I slink back to my seat, pulling my jacket lower. Nobody wants a stupid friend. Even Papi didn't want his stupid pudgy daughter. Just like he didn't want his stupid dropout son.

A student puts our morning math work face down on our desks. This teacher must grade papers during her lunch. That stinks. I flip it over. Well, la-di-da, guess what? Yep, another D. Well this day gets a D for Duh, doesn't it?

"Look, Sherie. She got a lower grade than you." Nancy grabs my paper and holds it up. "Didn't you learn anything at your old school?" she whispers to me.

"Yah," I whisper back, "I learned to do this." And I flick my pencil so it hits nosy Noodlenose right in her ear.

"DeeDee," says Mrs. Cruella. She motions me to the back table.

Great. I'm in trouble. But instead, she hands me a form with some boxes checked.

"These are the skills Yari will work on with you. I heard back from her teacher and you can start tomorrow. Her room is down the hall on the way to the lunchroom. We'll have someone walk you there."

"No, I can find it." I take the paper and stuff it in my desk. Does she think I'm stupid?

Well, duh. Yes she does.

CHAPTER THREE

D IS FOR DRAWING

I practically break down the door when I get home, rushing to get to the bathroom. And then I'm so thirsty I almost drink the whole gallon of juice. Danita fixes a snack and turns on the TV. I hide my new hoodie under my blanket.

Danita's phone rings. "It's Andrea," Danita says to me. "Sure, come over," she says to Andrea. "Nobody. Just DeeDee."

Nobody. Just DeeDee. That's my life.

Andrea and Danita eat and laugh about people I don't know. They gush over movie stars in a magazine that I can't see. They talk about Danita's quinceañera that I will not be going to.

"So, how many people will you invite?" I hear, and then I fall asleep. By the time I wake up, Mami is home and I smell dinner.

"*Te sientas bien?*" she asks me.

"Yah, I feel better. Just tired, " I say.

"Maybe you need to sleep in Danita room," she says.

"Maybe Danita needs to sleep on the couch," I argue. Who wants to sleep on a mattress on the floor? Not me.

"No, *mija*. She need her own room. She coming to be a woman. Fifteen."

Well, that's just fine, isn't it? For the millionth time I wish our trailer didn't burn down. Because even though I had a tiny room, it was my room, and my bed, and I didn't have to share it or sleep on somebody's floor.

"Go do homework. I cook favorite for you. *Gorditas para mi Gordita!*"

I want to tell Mami that until Papi comes home I'm not Mexican. No Mexican food. No Mexican nicknames. In fact, I wish I wasn't Mexican at all. One more reason I won't be going to Danita's annoying *quinceañera*, which is all she ever talks about.

But I'm starving and I love Mami's cooking. Just like Papi does. He always says that's why he married her. Because beauty doesn't last, but cooking does.

What do we love? Gorditas, for one. Mami's gorditas are sort of the same as the Hot Pockets they advertise on TV, but not sealed shut. They're a thousand times better. And we love *agua de horchata*, that rice drink with cinnamon sprinkled on the top. And crunchy, fried *buñuelos*. Who doesn't love those?

I use my new mechanical pencil to redo the incorrect math problems on my test, but I get the same answer as before. I guess I missed too many days of school. Papi used to help me with math even though he said he wasn't good in school. He hated the new way we learn to do it. "Numbers are numbers," he used to say. "Simple." And then he'd show me his way. Miss Hamilton said it was okay. Learn two ways and we shall be double smart, she used to say.

But Mrs. Cruella expects me to show my work. No shortcuts. Know what I say to that? LOL. Land O'Lakes. No more Papi. No more Papi's way. I do the problems two more times and get the same wrong answers. Whatever. I draw cats all around the edges of the math paper. Ugly cats. Cute cats. Big cats. Little cats. Maybe the answer is cats.

The smell of gorditas from the kitchen and the loud music from Danita's bedroom makes it hard to focus on my reading homework. I try, but the words start swimming and I suddenly remember I hid my accident pants under a towel in the bathroom. I dance to Danita's music all the way to the bathroom and all the way back. I throw the whole bundle in my dirty clothes bag.

Oh My Gatos! What stinks? Is it my dirty clothes? I quickly dance back to the bathroom and find some flowery smelling powder, then dump it in my dirty clothes bag to cover up the smell. FYI, I've never had an accident at school before, only when I'm sleeping, because I am a very sound sleeper. Mami says maybe those accidents are more frequent lately because of all the changes. The fire. The move. The new school. But she didn't say Papi. So I said it. And she started crying.

And I hate crying. That was the last time I talked to her about Papi.

I grab my sketchbook and my new pencil and open the sliding door to our little balcony. Across the open space I can see a building identical to ours. Every balcony has the same gray metal fence around it. Every balcony has the same metal porch light. Boring. What if they painted every fence a different color? I start counting balconies. Sixty. So sixty plus sixty equals one hundred twenty. Perfect. I start to sketch the balconies.

My almost-friend Jazzy has a crayon box with 120 different colors. One hundred twenty! But what's the best way to use those colors for the apartments? Keep the color shades together or scramble them? And how cool would it be to use a color name instead of a number for an apartment?

I practice answering someone who asks my address. "Well, yes. I live at Emerald Green North Ave. Unit Sky Blue or maybe Unit Macaroni and Cheese." That's the crayon I borrowed from Jazzy, BTW, and I really did mean to give it back, but then we moved. Sorry, Jazzy.

But what if you got stuck with a bad color name for your address? Burnt Umber. Or Asparagus.

"Well, I guess you should think twice about moving into a place with a bad color name, shouldn't you?" I say out loud to myself.

"What're you doing?" says a voice.

I whip around but I don't see anybody.

"Over here," says the voice.

And then I see the top of a hood on the balcony next to mine.

"Nothing. What're you doing?" I say.

"Watching you," says the voice.

"Why?"

"'Cause you're talking to yourself."

"So what did I say, then?" I ask.

"Think twice about moving into a place with a bad color name," says the kid.

"You've got big ears, then, don't you?" If there's one thing I hate, it's nosy people. Like Noodlenose Nancy. One more reason to miss my trailer. Nobody ever listened in on my private conversations.

"No, it's my cochlear implants. Kind of like hearing aids," says the kid.

"What?" I say.

"Cochlear implants, like hearing aids," says the kid, again.

"What?" I say again.

"That's funny. You're funny. Want to come over?"

I didn't mean to be funny. I meant to be annoying.

"Are you deaf?" I ask.

"Yes. I am. I can't hear you but I can answer your questions," says the kid.

"Ha. Now who's funny? What's your name?" It's hard to see in the Deep Space Sparkle evening light. That's another crayon color, BTW—from the Ultimate Crayon Collection.

"River," says the kid.

Just then, Danita opens the sliding door a crack. "DeeDee, what are you doing out here? Dinner's ready."

"I gotta go," I call to River in the dark and wave.

River puts up a hand to wave and instead separates four fingers into a V, and says, "Live long and prosper."

Live long and prosper? That's from *Star Trek*. My Papi's favorite show. "Why'd you say that?" I yell. But River's gone. *Star Trek weirdo*, I think.

•

I wake up on Tuesday morning and rush to take my second shower in eight hours. Yes, that's why, but everyone has accidents, don't they? I probably just drank too much water because I ate so many gorditas for dinner.

It's going to be a sparkly rainbow T-shirt day. I know it. First days—always rough. Second days—usually better. And today I might meet someone to walk with on the way to school.

But I don't see anyone. Just a few moms walking their kindergarten kids. But I do find room #13_ without any problems and I see DeeDee Diaz on a label above the coat hooks.

I hold my breath while Mrs. Cruella takes attendance. When she comes to my name, she stops and stares at me. We hold eyes for a second. Finally she says, "DeeDee Diaz?"

I breathe out. "Present," I say.

Before the tardy bell even rings, we're already knee-deep in the poetry unit. Then the groups share out. Noodlenose Nancy, of course, reads our group's cat poem. Everyone laughs when she turns the chart paper around. She's covered over my ugly cat with a piece of white paper and drawn five new cats with our names under each one. Hers has straight-arrow hair and wide oval eyes. Sherie's has short braids with barrettes. Nicole's wears glasses. Samantha's has blue eyes— Cornflower Blue. And the one with my name under it just happens to be a little fatter than the other four cats. I don't know if the class notices, but I notice.

I decide Jazzy is not at all like Nancy. Her magnet pulled us together. Nancy's vacuum pulls off parts of us. Mrs. Cruella hangs the poems on the wall. So I can see the fat cat all day.

While we're doing our independent reading, she puts my homework down on my desk. "I don't accept homework that's doodled on. Please erase this."

I hold up my pencil. No eraser. She points to a basket on the counter. "Use an eraser top until you can replenish your pencil supply."

I help myself to an eraser top for each of my chewed-up pencils. Perfect. I just replenished my supply.

Nancy whispers to Sherie, "Maybe we should donate some pencils to her."

I raise my hand. "Can I drink water?" I ask Mrs. Cruella.

"May I please get a drink of water?" she says to me.

"Yes, you may," I say right back. And I waltz out of the room. Nobody needs to feel sorry for me. A little, shimmery, pink purse sits on the shelf above the coat rack when I turn down the hall. It jingles when I slide it into my backpack.

I take my sweet time drinking water—really, really cold water and my even sweeter time walking back. They've started math when I return. Mrs. Cruella gives me a you-are-on-my-last-nerve-young-lady look. I stay awake by pinching myself and doodling tiny cats around the edges of my math book. I don't even like cats.

I'm first in line for recess and climb to the very top of the jungle gym. I sit there until I see the supervisors open the door to the lunchroom. Then I scramble down like a monkey and charge to the front of the line.

Yum. Pizza. I love pizza. Chocolate milk. I love chocolate milk.

I fill my tray and sit on the very edge of Room #13_'s table so only one person has to sit next to me.

"Move down," says the lunch supervisor, with a face like a mad bull. "Fill in the rest of the table."

So I scoot down and the table fills up around me. Everybody's talking and eating all at once. Sherie is saying, "Really? You're inviting all the girls?"

Nancy says, "That's what my mom said. Mani-pedis and we design our own bath bomb."

I think it's Hannah, the tiny one, who says, "Best birthday ever."

And Nancy says, "I know, right?"

I stuff the rest of my pizza in my mouth and dump my tray to go wait outside the bathroom. I stare at the Spring Fling poster again.

If only I had a bling thing to show off. Show everybody who I am. Find some friends who like what I like.

What do I like? Drawing? Not a Spring Fling kind of thing. Dancing? But Nancy always dances. What about skateboarding?

Before our trailer burned down, Danny's friend Freddie used to teach me some stuff on his board. How to position my feet and how to push and go pretty far without falling. He told me I was a natural. I've only practiced a little bit on my new skateboard because we stayed in a shelter until the Red Cross found our apartment. But there's plenty of time until March 19th to brush up and learn tricks. And I bet not many fourth graders try out to skate.

After lunch Mrs. Cruella walks us to the gym and we stop for a bathroom break. In gym, the teacher (with a chin like Mr. Incredible), tells us we're starting physical fitness testing. First we run laps but I have to stop before his stopwatch. Then we lie down on the floor for sit ups. Mr. Incredible shakes his head when he sees I can barely do one.

Before the next test I go get a drink and he says, "Permission needed," and points to a list of rules next to the gym door.

I EXPECT:

YOUR BEST PERFORMANCE

YOUR POSITIVE ATTITUDE

YOUR REQUEST FOR PERMISSION TO LEAVE YOUR STATION.

I bet this is what it was like for Danny in the National Guard. I almost give him a salute.

On the way back to class, I ask Mrs. Cruella for permission to use the bathroom. "May I please use the restroom?" I say.

"DeeDee, we already had a bathroom break."

Noodlenose Nancy whispers something to Sherie and they giggle. I get back in the line. Forget it. But from now on Sherie will be Despicable Me Sherie.

When Mrs. Cruella calls the first group of students to read at the back table she says, "DeeDee, you can head to peer tutoring. Do you need help finding room 118?"

I shake my head no. Does she have to announce to everybody how stupid I am? I visit the bathroom first and get a big drink of really, really cold water. Then I wander down the lunchroom hallway to find room #118. Do I knock? Do I wait? What will I do in peer tutoring, anyway?

A kid comes out of the room. He reads the paper in my hand, then sticks his head back in the room. "Get Yari," he tells another kid.

A few minutes later, a very smiley girl with big white teeth bounces out the door.

"Hi! Mr. Barker told me I'm tutoring again. My other kid moved." She leads me to a room near the computer lab, where a few pairs of kids sit close together. I give her the paper from Mrs. Cruella and look at her outfit out of the corner of my eye. Cute jeans and a flowery top that flutters around her. Over that she's wearing a jackety thing, with gathers in the back. I feel super ugly in my sparkly rainbow T-shirt spotted with chocolate milk.

"Nobody told me you started yesterday," says Yari. "I'm the team leader on the Student Leadership Team. I'm supposed to show the new kids around."

"It's okay. I've moved around a lot," I say.

"Me too. But I've been here since third grade. Don't worry. You'll catch up. Mrs. Krewell always thinks bilingual kids are behind because they speak Spanish. So sad, *qué lástima*." Yari giggles and rolls her eyes. "Not too many bilingual kids go to Frosty."

I smile at her nickname for Robert Frost. "You speak Spanish?" I ask, sounding silly.

"*Claro que sí*. Of course. I'm Mexican, are you? And I love your T-shirt, by the way. I'm all about bling," she says. "Let's look at your skills check list." She studies it for a minute. "Mrs. Krewell put down that you're using the old method of multiplying. That's the way my dad tried to teach me. He got so mad about the new way to do math."

"My dad, too," I say. I don't say he's in Mexico.

"Well, they have parent workshops here to explain the new way to do math. Even my dad learned the new way. We moved here because of my dad," Yari says. "So he didn't have to drive so far to work."

"Me, too," I lie. I don't say we haven't seen Papi for nine weeks and three days. I know. I counted.

Yari has a bracelet made of colored string braids knotted together around her wrist. Red, blue, green, orange, and yellow. I wonder if she made it herself. I wonder if she'll make me one.

•

After I get home from school and have my snack, I go out on my balcony again. It's chilly-nice and still sunny. I see a boy making a chalk drawing of a dragon. It stretches from the parking lot all the way to the balcony next to mine. It reminds me of the design on my skateboard. I watch while the kid draws fire shooting from the dragon's mouth. Then he looks up and waves.

"Hi again," he says. "You never told me your name."

It's River, the kid from the balcony yesterday. The Star Trek weirdo. Today his hood is off and I see his long, shiny-black, curly-noodle hair. When he tilts his head up I can see plastic things behind his ears.

"DeeDee."

"Come help me," he says.

"I can't. My mom isn't home." It's an excuse. I'm sure Mami wouldn't care, but I'm still not too sure about this kid.

"Well, that's highly illogical," River calls up to me. "That's from *Star Trek*. Dr. Spock."

"I know. My dad loves *Star Trek.*"

"My dad used to love it, too. He was a Trekkie."

"See you later," I call down, wondering why his dad isn't a Trekkie anymore.

"Live long and prosper," River says and does the Vulcan salute. "That's actually a Jewish blessing. Did you know that?"

I go in and close the balcony door, trying to separate my third and fourth finger to do my own Vulcan salute. It's not that easy. "Live long and prosper," I whisper to nobody, hoping Papi hears me far away in Mexico.

CHAPTER FOUR

D IS FOR DRAMA

I hear pounding on the bathroom door.

"DeeDee, get out," Queen Bee yells. "You're not the only one who lives here. Mami, make her get out. We have to leave before she does."

I was just about to get out, but now I find a few more drops to towel off and sneak some of her Big and Sexy hair gel and a dab of Cristiano Ronaldo perfume. Then I waltz out.

"Mami, DeeDee stinks like a boy!" Danita yells.

Mami pads down the hall in her slippers. She sniffs. *"Gordita, la colonia de Daniel."*

Oh My Gatos. Daniel's cologne? Why do these things happen to me? I try to get back in the bathroom to wash it off, but Danita laughs and locks the door.

My head starts to hurt as I'm stuffing the wet sheets in the laundry and picking out my clothes. The smell from the laundry and the cologne slam into me and I rush to the kitchen and barf in the garbage. I feel terrible. I sit down on the couch and lean my head on the armrest.

The next thing I know Mami is feeling my forehead. "*Pobrecita.* You have a fever."

"Uh." Staying home from school is no fun if you feel lousy. Such a waste of a great day.

"Take these." She gives me two purple pills. "Go to sleep. I will tell Daniel to be careful of you while I clean this morning."

I don't correct her. I know what she means. She cleans houses besides working at Papa Giapino's Pizza. And Danny won't be happy he has to take care of me, little baby DeeDee who can't take even take care of herself.

The TV is blaring the next time I wake up, and I don't see Danny anywhere. I'm starving. I eat a bowl of Cinnamon Toast Crunch with a banana and some squirty whip cream I find in the door of the fridge. I love that stuff. Papi used to squirt it into my mouth, like I was a baby bird.

"What are you doing up?" Danny says, coming in the front door.

"Where were you?"

"Just outside."

I smell cigarettes and know why he was outside.

"Does Mami know you smoke?"

"Don't tell. It's just one."

"Well, it stinks."

"That's not me." He sniffs me. "Is that my cologne? Yikes, this whole room stinks." He opens the closet and coughs. "Gross. It's this laundry."

I hug my arms around myself tight. I'm so ashamed. I'm stinking up the whole apartment.

Danny pulls out the laundry basket and I see my new-to-me skateboard from the Secret Swap. Someone painted glittery purple flames, blowing from a pink dragon's mouth, and a bright yellow lightning bolt shooting from a turquoise cloud. And it's got brand new grip tape, even though the trucks are flattened a bit from previous grinding. I know the design will wear off once I start really cruising. But it's amazing anyway.

Freddie, Danny's old friend, told me I needed a skateboard with a smaller deck than his. And my new-to-me board is perfect. Danita told me to lose weight so I'll have better balance. And to exercise so my core gets stronger. Whatever, Flaquita-Danita. Like I'm an apple or something.

I'll have to start practicing if I decide to sign up for Spring Fling, but where? The apartment hallway, with its buckled carpet? The parking lot, with its cars and speed bumps? The sidewalk between the apartment buildings has a sign: NO BIKES, ROLLERBLADES, OR SKATEBOARDS. Maybe Danny knows where a skatepark is.

"Do you ever see Freddie anymore?" I ask Danny. I know Freddie and Danny dropped out of high school together and Danny lived in Freddie's trailer for a while. Because Papi got so over-my-dead-body-mad about Danny dropping out.

"Nope," says Danny, making the p sound very loudly. I don't think he's friends with Freddie anymore. "Come on. I've got my uniform to wash. Do you feel good enough to go?" He pulls the stinky laundry bag to the door and puts it in our wheelie cart. Then he puts his duffle bag over his shoulder and carries the laundry basket from the bathroom. "Can you pull the cart?"

My fingers are frozen and my toes are numb when we dump everything on the floor in front of the washers at Rub-a-Dub-Tub. I guess Danny knows what he's doing when it comes to laundry. He gives me dollars for the change machine and I put the quarters in the slots while he loads the washers.

"Where did you learn to do laundry?"

"NGYCP. National Guard Youth Challenge Program."

"Really? They teach you how to do laundry?" I repeat the letters in my head. NGYCP.

"Yep. We rotate jobs. I can cook, too. Life coping skills. One of the eight core components we have to master to graduate."

"Ooh. Bet all the girls want to go out with you."

Danny punches me, not even hard, but I'm so unsteady I fall into a chair.

"You okay?" He looks at me. "Whoa. You don't look good."

The washers chug around and around and the detergent smell is flowery and soapy. It's moisty-warm and I'm sweating. My legs are sooo tired. Everything is foggy with Cristiano Ronaldo cologne. "I'm thirsty."

Danny buys me an orange soda and sits down next to me.

"I'm not friends with Freddie anymore. I have new friends now," he says. "Friends from NGYCP. Good friends."

"Oh," I say. "I met some girls at my school."

"Friends?"

"I don't know. One of them is really nice. Yari." I don't tell Danny that Yari is my peer tutor. Kids can be friends with their peer tutors, can't they? "And one of them is sort of mean."

Danny says, "Remember how Papi always said '*el que anda con lobos, aprende aullar*,' one who walks with wolves, learns to howl?"

"Uh-huh." I remember, but I never understood.

"He was right. Stick up for yourself. Don't follow along and let the other wolves change who you are." He pats my hand and goes to switch the laundry to the dryer.

I doze off watching the swishing, rainbow-colored clothes, and *Llena de Amor*, an old telenovela, which if you don't know is about a girl whose mother dies and she goes to live with her relatives. She dresses cute, has tons of friends, and she's on the plump side, which I guess is fine for TV stars, but not for regular ten-year-olds. And not for Mami either. She always worries about her *masitas*. Papi says he loves her just the way she is, but does she wonder if that's still true now that Papi went away?

I sigh. I don't want tons of friends. Just one or two who don't care whether I speak Spanish or not and if my belly is too porky. I think about River. The Star Trek Weirdo next door. Is that what he wants too? One or two friends who don't care if he's a little weird?

As the show is ending, I decide to go on a diet and dress cute. It seems to be working for Marianela, star of *Llena de Amor*, and Yari too. But not until after lunch, which Danny brings me from Burger King.

"Feel better?" he asks as I polish off the very last little scrap of a french fry.

"Don't you have to go to work?"

"In a while. Mami says you can stay alone until Danita gets home."

The laundry takes us two hours, start to finish, which is not too bad, but still a waste of time. If I ruled the world, I'd invent spot-disappearing spray so clothes would never get dirty. It could work on dog poop, too. Spray and poof! Gone. It might work on bossy sisters, and Noodlenoses, but it's not been tested. LOL. Laugh Out Loud not Land O'Lakes.

We trudge home, our neat little stacked bundles of clothes and sheets bouncing up and down in the wheelie cart. I feel dizzy.

Danny gets to the apartment door just as a yellow bus pulls up and River jumps out.

"So we meet again, DeeDee," he says as he rushes to open the door for us.

My vision is blurry, but it looks like his fingers are fused together, with a split down the middle in a permanent Vulcan salute. No, that can't be. It's just my eyes.

"Thanks," Danny says. "I'm Daniel Diaz, Danny."

"I'm River."

Suddenly River goes all black and blurry and I start to tilt. I'm not like a character in a movie that faints gracefully and melts slowly to a crumply heap on the ground. Nuh-uh. Not me. Crash. There goes the wheelie cart. Whoosh. There goes the laundry. Splat. There goes River. Thud. There goes me. And just before my head hits the concrete step I have a thought: River will never ask me to come over again.

CHAPTER FIVE

D IS FOR DISEASE

I wake up lying in bed with a long, plastic bendy straw in my arm, still worrying about the laundry. Did Danny clean everything up? Does River think I'm weird? Is there blood on the sidewalk? Gross. I can hear voices outside my door. Not really my door. The door to this room. The room where people who drop dead go. This is probably the waiting room for heaven. And I'm disappointed. I imagined heaven would be more colorful and smell better.

And what am I wearing? No angel wings, that's for sure. Some sort of apron that opens in the back. A nightgown without any buttons to keep it shut. I guess heaven doesn't have my size wings. They probably don't get a lot of kids. I peek under the sheet and see my pudgy tummy, but no blood. That's when I figure I'm not in heaven but a hospital.

The voices are clearer. I hear Mami speaking in fast Spanish with lots of *¡Ayes!* Then Danny in English. Then another voice. Then Danny in Spanish. Arguing, I realize. Arguing about what? Me. That's what. They're arguing about me. I hear the letter K, over and over. Then I can pick out three letters: DKA. The door opens.

"Gordita!" Mami rushes to my side and slobbers me with kisses.

A tall lady with very curly black hair piled up on her head like a fountain spray squeezes my toes. "Glad you decided to join us," she says.

"I don't remember deciding," I say back. "What happened?" I'm not sure if she's a nurse or a doctor, but I kind of like the way she talks straight to me.

"I'm Dr. Ferreyra. And I'm very glad to see you awake. We think you passed out because of diabetic ketoacidosis. Big word. Means too much sugar in your blood, not enough insulin."

Mami blows her nose. Is she crying? Will I die? Is that what those big words mean?

"*Es mi culpa, mija.*" She pats me. "My fault. I should know you sick."

"No, no. It's no one's fault." Dr. Ferreyra puts her hand on Mami's shoulder. "Diabetes is a sneaky disease. The body tries really hard to fix itself, and that can fool moms, and doctors, too. But you'll get better and learn to boss this disease around," she says, turning back to me.

My brain is spinning, spinning, spinning. Whoa. Whoa. Whoa. Stop. I have a disease? I probably caught it at Robert Frost. I knew I didn't like that new school. I pull away from Mami and put both hands over my mouth. I might be contagious. Did I give it to Danny? He hasn't moved an inch. Only his jaw muscle is twitching. What's wrong with everybody?

Dr. Ferreyra walks around the bed and sits on the window ledge. Sunlight pours through the window and I squint at her. "Oh, sorry," she says and pulls the blinds down. Now there are stripes of sunlight across her face, giving her a zebra-face. And it's very distracting.

"So, DeeDee, first of all, most people with diabetes live perfectly normal lives once they take control of the disease. Second, it's not something that's contagious. It will help me a lot if you can tell me about any change in the way you've been feeling lately." Dr. Zebra-Face crosses her arms and waits for me to talk.

How does she know I didn't catch it? In fact how does she know I have some disease? It might be the flu. Maybe an allergic reaction to Danny's cologne. I try mind control on Danny. Look at me. Look at me. Look at me. But he stares out the window with his hands in his pockets.

"Danny," I yell.

He jumps and turns his head.

"Danny, tell her I'm fine. I just got tired. That's all."

Danny turns and his face is a thunderstorm. "And that's my fault, isn't it? I shouldn't have made you walk. Shouldn't have taken you out."

"Oh My Gatos! What is wrong with everybody? I just caught the flu. I'll be fine. I feel fine." But I am thirsty. I swing my legs over the edge of the bed to go find a drinking fountain, then remember I have a big window on my backside and a plastic snake in my arm.

"*Mija. Descansa*, rest." Mami pushes me gently and pulls the sheet up over me.

"*Tome agua*, drink water," I whisper to her. I forget all about not speaking Spanish until Papi comes home.

"Thirsty?" Dr. Zebra-Face pushes a button on the side of my bed and a man bustles in, wearing a bright flowered shirt and pants the same periwinkle blue as my weird apron, as if he's a Hawaiian surfer dude.

"Well, my goodness. You're awake!" he says and checks the bag attached to my IV.

"I'm Seigan, your nurse." Mr. Hawaii slaps a black band on my arm and pumps it up. "Look, I can pump you up." I know he's making a joke, but I don't laugh. I don't like people doing stuff to me before they tell me, including taking my blood pressure and putting plastic tubes in my arm. And poking me with needles is off limits. You can ask every nurse who ever tried it.

"Seigan, could we get a meal brought up? Diabetic Diet-Consistent CHO? And some water?" says Dr. Zebra-Face.

"As you wiiissshhhhh," he says. "Let me get a quick reading before dinner. Just a tiny prick on your finger, my lady." And he moves so fast I don't even respond. He squeezes my finger so tightly I hardly feel the poke. My mind is like a dull pencil, blurry and muddled. But my family's sad faces make me want to pretend I'm okay. Mr. Hawaii grabs a few things off the tray table next to my bed and slips them into his pocket. Then he's off.

"I hope dinner is gorditas!" I whisper to Mami to make her smile.

"Nope, I'm pretty sure it will be chicken." The doctor wrinkles her nose. "At least, the first meal usually is."

Chicken. Chicken makes me think of Papi. He loves *pollo al carbon*. On the grill. Or from *El Pollo Hermanos*. And when my chicken comes, I wish it was Papi's juicy, crunchy, charcoal chicken instead of the dry, stick-in-my-throat, Styrofoam chicken on my tray.

•

Mami never leaves me all afternoon, dozing in a chair with a footrest. Danny goes home and comes back with

Danita. The Queen Bee brings me a new teddy bear from the hospital gift shop. I pretend it's the cutest thing since Shawn Mendes, since I know she's trying to be nice, but it's very stiff with pink fur so thin I can see bare skin. That's a joke. Bare skin, bearskin. Get it?

I don't say anything to Danita about the ugly bear because I don't want to make trouble. I've already caused enough today. And her being nice to me isn't going to change my mind about her *quinceañera*. Especially if Papi isn't going to be there.

We all sit and watch the TV that's mounted to my ceiling, and pretend the interrupting nurses and strange beeping noises are perfectly normal and we're having more fun than a barrel of monkeys. And I pretend to be cheery and brave, even though I'd rather be going over Niagara Falls in a barrel with a monkey. When Danita stands up, her Passion-Pink lip gloss falls from her pocket and I quickly cover it with my hand.

"Did you call my teacher?" I'm worried. I'm already behind according to Mrs. Cruella. And I hope they don't assign a different kid for Yari to work with. I slide the Passion-Pink lip gloss under my sheet.

"*Mañana*," Mami says. "Your homework?"

"Can one of your friends bring it to the apartment or to the hospital?" Danny asks.

"I'm not sure if anyone lives near me." The truth is I'm not sure I have any friends. And especially not the kind of friends you'd expect to visit you in the hospital. Not best friends.

Maybe if I had had a little more time with Yari . . . I know she's the kind of person who'd visit a friend in the hospital. And so am I. If I had a best friend I'd climb two hundred mountains and cross a wild river to bring them homework.

River's face flashes in my memory. I hope I never see him again. Talk about embarrassing. And he probably feels the same way after I catapulted him over. I don't just have a disease. I may as well be a disease.

Before Mr. Hawaii's shift is over, he tells me if I'm lucky I might get a visit from one of the student nurses doing their clinicals. Whatever that means. Sure enough, a nurse who looks like she's Danita's age comes to check on me, smiling a lot at Danny. She changes the bag of saltwater that's attached to my arm and checks my blood pressure again.

I pay attention when she whips out a baby remote control like the one that turns our ceiling fan on and off and puts it on the table next to me, along with a little round container. So that's what Mr. Hawaii put in his pocket before he left. She reaches for my finger, wipes it off, and holds what looks like a flash drive up to it. I wonder if she's hooking me up to a computer or something. All of a sudden the flash drive pokes me. I scream bloody murder. It didn't hurt like this when Mr. Hawaii poked me.

"DeeDee, DeeDee, *cálmate*," begs Mami.

I scream louder and the student nurse looks scared. I hope she starts crying. I hope she quits nursing school. I hope she gets fired.

"I'm so sorry, I must have hit a nerve ending. I thought she knew what to expect. I'm so sorry," says the nurse.

"She's such a baby," Danita tells Mama. "Make her stop."

"Well, how'd you like it? Maybe we should stick you," Danny lashes out at Danita.

I keep screaming.

Suddenly nurses are filling up my room. Shushing me. Offering me popsicles. And peppermints. Books and balloons.

Danny sits on my bed and takes my hand. "Where does it hurt, *mija*?" He bends his head closer and places my finger on his lips.

I stop screaming. I'm shaking and my throat hurts.

The student nurse holds up the remote control. "I didn't know. I thought . . ."

"She has fear for needles," Mami explains.

It turns out the remote control is a blood glucose monitor—a glucometer—and the flash drive is a finger poker. Inside the little round container are the test strips. And now I remember Mr. Hawaii using it, but he was so fast and I was so woozy, I didn't pay attention.

And it turns out, the nurses tell me, that the thing that I hate most is the thing that will save my life. That little drop of blood is like weather radar, watching for activity that might cause my body to have a diabetic crash. Blink. Blink. Warning, the numbers say, bad storm glucose reading. Or blink, blink, all is calm, all is well. And that's why they stick me three more times in the night. I scream every time. Mami gets up from her recliner chair to calm me down.

In the morning one more nurse pops in, takes my blood pressure, and says, "So, you're the screamer," as if I'm famous all over the hospital. I should be embarrassed, making such a scene over a little finger prick. But I hate blood. I hate needles. I hate people messing with me. So I don't even care.

Mami doesn't want to leave me, but when Mr. Hawaii starts his shift he promises to take good care of me. "My precious," he jokes in a weird voice. I think from Lord of the Rings.

"Be good, Dinora," says Mami.

"Tell Danny to pick me up. I'm coming home. And that's the truth."

"Maybe tomorrow or the next day," says Mr. Hawaii. "Your readings are all over the place. We need to watch your diet and get you stable. And you have a lot to learn before you go home." He reaches for my finger and I wrench my hands away and stuff them under the sheet.

I glare at Mami. She looks so tired. I almost say *I love you, Mami,* but I'm too mad. I know she's thinking about calling in sick to stay with me, but then she gives a sad little wave and deserts me. Just like Papi. Leaving me all alone in the hospital with Mr. Hawaii.

CHAPTER SIX

D IS FOR DISTINCTION

Mr. Hawaii puts his face close to mine. "You can't handle the truth." I know he's doing one of his movie quotes. I ignore him. He doesn't move. "But I'm going to tell you the truth. Diabetes is no fun." He gets even closer and his voice gets louder. "But, we all want you to live so we're going to keep trying to take care of you. Will that be okay?"

"Yes," I say in a tiny voice.

"Okay." He stands up. "So, now that you're done feeling sorry for yourself, I'm going to train you to survive." Mr. Hawaii puts the flash drive to his own finger and explains how it works. A tiny drop of blood pops out at the end of his finger.

He puts the flash drive on my bedside table and pulls an orange from his pocket. "Here. Practice on my friend Orlando Orange first. Whenever you're ready. I'm not just the greatest—I'm the double greatest glucose-monitoring trainer this side of the Mississippi. And don't make a liar out of me."

You have got to be kidding me. He wants me to stab my own finger? I can't stand needles. I can't stand pain. And I can't stand blood. Three important reasons why I can't have diabetes. Diabetes can just pick somebody else—somebody who enjoys watching their diet and poking themselves with needles. Mr. Hawaii waits for me to take the orange. Oh all right. I take it and aim the device into its dimply peel. Click. No juice comes pouring out like I expected.

I'm just about to stab it again when there's a knock. Another nurse, probably, to pick up my tray, check if I peed, or take my blood pressure.

"Speak, friend, and enter," Mr. Hawaii says in a different movie voice. I roll my eyes. "What?" he says. "You don't like Lord of the Rings?"

A skinny kid slides into the room. "I can speak friend," he says. "Mellon. That's friend in Sindarin. It's from Lord of the Rings." It's River. He's the color of the Tumbleweed crayon in the set of 120. A little darker than me when I'm outside a lot.

"Friend of yours?" asks Mr. Hawaii.

River holds up his hand and greets me with the Vulcan salute. "Remember me?" he asks.

"*Star Trek*," says Mr. Hawaii. "Live long and prosper."

Good Gatos. They're both weirdos. And of course I remember River. It's not easy to forget smashing someone onto the concrete. I stare at the hand that saluted me. No wonder it's easy for River to copy the Vulcan salute. His fingers are stuck together, like I thought I imagined before I fainted, with a split between fingers number three and four.

"If you don't mind, Dr. Spock, Diva Dee is just about to show off her new talent for checking her glucose to manage her diabetes." He puts a new lancet in the device and hands it to me. "Float like a butterfly. Sting like a bee."

And I'm trapped.

"Hey," I say to River. "Want to watch?" I flare my nostrils at Mr. Hawaii, just to let him know that the game is on. Watch your back, Surfer Dude. I grit my teeth. I can't tell whether my head or my hand is shaking. I want to close my eyes, but that would be a mistake. I might poke into an important artery and bleed to death.

River stands very still with his hand on the edge of my bed. "It's okay," he whispers. "Breathe."

I take a deep breath and let it out. Click. A tiny dot of scarlet appears. I don't scream. In fact, I barely feel the prick, maybe because I'm expecting it or concentrating so hard.

"Ladies and gentlemen. I give you, Diva Dee the Wonder Girl. Draws blood on her first attempt. And her amazing trainer, Nurse Seigan." He changes his voice. "It's hard to be humble when you're as great as I am." Then he quickly takes the little remote control—the glucometer—and dabs my finger on the piece of paper on the end. He reads the numbers on the little screen. "Hmmm. What did they bring you for breakfast?"

I point to the breakfast tray and make a barfing noise. I'm surprised when River laughs.

"Ah-ha. You already peeked, didn't you? So, you don't care for gourmet hospital food? What can I say? Problem is, your diet is your friend. Eating is no longer a matter of love and like, but life and death." Mr. Hawaii swings the tray in front of me. "Ooh, we've got the cold watery egg and the dry toast, have we? I think I can rustle up some better grub. And what about your friend? Can I bring you something?"

"Those breakfast potatoes with ketchup?" River's voice has a funny accent. Sort of like talking with your fingers pinching your nose and dropping off the endings of words. Then he adds, "And cranberry apple juice, no ice."

Me and Mr. Hawaii can't believe it. "A regular, huh?" he asks River.

River nods and moves some curly-noodle hair so we can see his ears. I recognize the white, plastic-looking device I saw before. Sort of like a funny-shaped Bluetooth attached to both ears with a wire connected to a knob on his head.

"Cochlear implants," River says. Then he holds up his two-finger hands. "And plastic surgery."

"Wait, are you the famous ectrodactyly patient?" asks Mr. Hawaii.

"Me, that might be," River says in a Yoda voice and winks.

Mr. Hawaii reaches out and shakes River's two-finger hand. He bows his head. "It's an honor to meet you," he says in a deep voice.

"No, the honor is mine," River says, trying to go even deeper with his voice.

They both laugh. "Matrix," they say at the same time. I roll my eyes.

Mr. Hawaii turns to me. "River's quite a celebrity at Westmont Hospital. A real inspiration. Now, if you'll excuse me"—he opens the door—"I'll be back." And this time even I know he's imitating The Terminator.

Mr. Hawaii zips out the door and right back in to collect the glucometer and the lancing device. "Just in case you decide to poke more holes in yourself, Diva Dee. And by the way, Orlando and I will be back later to teach you how to give injections."

I can't help myself. I know lines from movies, too. "Let it go, let it go!"

Mr. Hawaii pokes his head in again and smiles. "Frozen. Some people are worth melting for."

"He's nuts," says River.

"Look who's talking." I make a funny face at him. "What're you doing here, anyway?" I wonder if he keeps his hair long to cover his hearing aids. And what makes him so skinny. He even has a skinny nose. Maybe it's his health problems.

"I came to visit you. And I brought you this." He holds out a drawing. "It's you—when you said you wanted to live in apartment Sky Blue, unit Macaroni and Cheese." A girl with long, brown, wavy hair stands on a balcony facing a background of balconies, all colors and designs. Some have stripes, some have swirls, and one definitely has yellow macaroni and cheese on it. It's really awesome but I'm a little embarrassed. It's like he read my mind or something.

"Cool," I say, thinking it's nice to have someone visit besides family.

"Yah. My mom dropped me off early, before my audiologist appointment," he says.

"Oh." Okay, I admit I'm one tiny bit let down River isn't here just to visit me. Then I tell myself to get a grip. We're not even friends. He's just my neighbor. A Star Trek weirdo.

Some people, Mami for one, would think it's rude to ask River about his fingers. But don't you want to know? And you're not here, so it's up to me. "What happened to your fingers and why are you an inspiring celebrity?" He doesn't have to answer if he doesn't want to.

He sits down on the edge of my bed and rolls one hand around the other. Over and over. Like he's washing them without soap and water. Under his breath I hear him say, "I hate it when people say I'm inspiring."

I look closer at his hands. Both hands have a split down the middle with one strangely shaped finger on each side of the split. A scar runs from the point of the V into the palm of his hands. Another smaller scar surrounds one of his thumbs and it sticks out at an angle. Whoa! Must have been a car accident. Or a fire. Maybe Mr. Hawaii will tell me if River doesn't.

"Long story or short?" River says

"What?"

"My fingers."

"It's your story, you decide."

"Birth defect. It's called ectrodactyly. Inherited. Only happens to one baby in ninety thousand. Which makes me very distinct."

"And why did Mr. Hawaii call you famous?"

"Mr. Hawaii?"

"You know, Nurse Seigan, with the Hawaiian shirt."

"Oh. Well, people with ectrodactyly often also have hearing loss. I'm one of the hospital's first patients to have a digit reconstruction and cochlear implants. Another distinction."

So his fingers and his ears are messed up? And he was born that way? And he calls it distinct? I'd say stink is a better word. And it stinks I've got diabetes. And it stinks my friend Sandro's little sister has a heart problem.

Papi must have known. He didn't want a daughter with a disease. I wonder if everybody's parents feel that way. But I don't ask River. Instead I ask, "What are cochlear implants? Hearing aids?"

"No, not hearing aids. Hearing aids just magnify the sounds. It's very technical. Sure you want to know?"

"Does a bear poop in the woods?" I hold up my pink bear. "Yes, I want to know."

"Okay. Well, the implants have lots of parts. The microphone picks up the sounds and sends them to the speech processor," River points at the Bluetooth thingy around his ear. "Then the transmitter and receiver send the code to the electrodes they put inside my inner ear and then it goes to my brain along the hearing nerve. You got all that? " River smiles. "Any questions?"

"Whoa. I might need a drawing. So were you deaf before the implants? And is everything normal now?"

"Not completely deaf. But hearing aids didn't do much. And now I can hear, but it's probably not exactly normal. I still have to read lips sometimes. And I couldn't talk very well. Now I sound almost normal, don't I?"

I don't want to be rude, but it does take a while to get used to the way he talks. "Almost, except for your endings," I say, careful about hurting his feelings and surprised with myself for worrying about it.

"I'm working on that at my school, with my speech therapist."

"What school?"

"Learning Center for the Deaf. It's in Duarton."

"Everybody's deaf and dumb? The whole school?"

"I can't believe you just said that."

"What?"

"Saying deaf and dumb is rude. Nobody says it anymore."

"My brother says it. 'Don't be deaf and dumb, DeeDee.'"

River grabs the remote from my tray table and clicks off the TV. He squeezes his fingers together. He looks mad.

"I didn't mean stupid-dumb," I say quickly. "I meant people who have trouble talking. You know, hearing impaired, or hearing disabled?" I'm not sure what the right words are. I never thought about this before. "No deaf kids went to any of the schools I went to," I add.

"See," River says. "This is the problem with all the deaf kids at one school. You don't know a single deaf person. We aren't hearing-impaired or hearing disabled. We're hard of hearing. There's nothing impairing us or disabling us. Nobody says you're pancreas-impaired or pancreas-disabled because you have diabetes."

"I didn't say it to be mean. If you can't hear, aren't you disabled?"

"If you came to my school you'd feel disabled. You wouldn't be able to talk to anybody because you don't speak sign language. You wouldn't even know how to ask to use the bathroom in Miss Swanson's class, because she's deaf. And following directions would be impossible for you, so good luck figuring out what the homework assignments are."

"Okay, I get it." Oh My Gatos. I'm sorry I said anything.

River keeps talking. "So you'd have to able yourself. You'd have to learn sign language. And to read lips. To pay attention to lights, not bells. Just like we do." He sounds really irritated with me, as though I just dissed his favorite soccer team or insulted his mother. "I have distinctions that make me unique. Everybody does. They're not handicaps."

"Well, I'm sorry. I didn't know." I'm getting a little annoyed. I'm the one in the hospital. I'm the one who's got diabetes. I'm the one he's visiting. How dare he turn off my TV? I almost say, Oh My Gatos. Excuse me for living. But I don't, because he starts talking again.

His voice is softer now. He sounds almost sorry he got so upset. "Don't worry about it. You're not the only one. A lot of people don't even care to learn. The three ways to label people who can't hear are 'hard of hearing,' like me, 'deaf' with a lowercase 'd,' like my friends who can't hear sounds, and 'Deaf' with a capital 'D' for the Deaf community."

"Oh," I say, nodding my head, deciding I want to be one of the people who care to learn. Papi always wants to learn. He reads all the time. Whenever I'm stubborn about doing homework he says, "*Loro viejo no aprende a hablar.*" The old parrot can't learn to talk. Then he says, "*Mi Lora Hermosa,*" and gives me a hug. I wish Papi would visit me in the hospital.

What if I never see him again? I stare at my hands. The hospital ID bracelet hangs loose on my wrist. Diaz, Dinora. Diabetic. DOB: 12/10/2008. Westmont Hospital. I close my eyes to stop them from watering.

"I'm going to transfer to a regular school," River says, interrupting my thinking.

"Why?"

"Lots of reasons. Too many little kids. Only me and two others in fourth grade. And we don't have art or music teachers."

"No art and music? Those are my favorite classes."

"Also, I want to experience being in a hearing learning environment. And I hate the bus. I'd rather walk to Robert Frost."

Robert Frost? That's my school. I don't say what I should say. I go to Robert Frost. We might be in the same class. We could walk to school together. I know I should say it, and I know I'm a brat. It's not because of his—distinctions. Well, it partly is, but not completely. It's also his *Star Trek* talk and his big words. He's kind of a geek, isn't he? What if Noodlenose saw us walking to school together? I can just see how she would make fun of River. And me, if she thought we were friends. You know you would feel the same way. He's better off staying at his hard-of-hearing school.

"How did they get those electrodes inside your ear? Did it hurt?" I say after a bit.

"Not really. They knock you out. Then they cut your ear open from the back. I have a scar." He pulls up the transmitter so I can see, but I don't look. You know how I am about needles and blood. "I didn't even have to spend the night. But it doesn't work right away. You wait until everything heals and then start the device."

The door opens and Mr. Hawaii is back. He sets down two trays. "For you, Diva Dee, whole wheat pancakes with strawberries and low-fat whipped cream. And for you, Distinguished River, potatoes with ketchup and juice. Will there be anything else, my lady?"

The smell of the pancakes makes me appreciate Mr. Hawaii, just a little. If I have to be here, I guess I'm glad he's my nurse. "Thanks," I tell him. "I'll be in touch."

I watch River fix up his potatoes with his two-finger hands. He holds the ketchup packet between the two big sections of his right hand, and pulls the tab open with his left. Then he picks up the fork using his whole fist and starts shoveling potatoes into his mouth. "What?" he says when he notices me watching.

"I don't know how you did that." I open the syrup packet, imagining how hard it would be without all my fingers.

"Well, nobody knows they're different until they try to live in a world made for people without congenital anomalies." He holds up his hands. "That's what they call these. Take this ketchup packet for example." He picks up the used packet. "Just a little larger tab on the end would make about a thousand people's lives much easier."

"I never thought about that. Do you get mad at stuff?"

"Sometimes. But it's always been like this for me, so I never knew any different. Glad I had surgery, though." He wiggles his right hand fingers. "Ready for some big words?"

"Hit me," I say.

"The transposition of my index metacarpal with reconstruction of my thumb web space makes things much easier." He points to the scar running toward his palm.

"Oh My Gatos. How do you even say those words?"

He wiggles his thumb on the other hand. "And this wasn't here. Can you keep a secret?"

"Cross my heart." And there it is again. The thought that I don't want to hurt his feelings. That we might be starting to be friends.

"It used to be my big toe."

"Seriously? Your toe is your thumb?" I take a closer look. You'd never know.

"You're the first person I told."

"So did those surgeries hurt?"

"I was a baby for the first two, but my mom tells me I didn't like them very much. When they cleaned up the scar tissue last year, I figured out why. Yowzers." He pushes the juice glass to the edge of the tray so he can pick it up. "When are you going home?"

"Not soon enough. I have to be stable, whatever that means."

"Where's your mom? Mine always stayed with me."

Well, la-di-da, I think. Not all of us have perfect lives. Just when I think we might be starting to be friends he gets all high and mighty. I'm about to tell him to mind his own beeswax. Then I remember Danny. So worried. And Mami. So sad. Plus stabilizing diabetes is probably not half as bad as River's surgeries.

So I just act nice. "My mom and my brother have to work. My dad . . ." I stop. I have not told anybody about my papi. But River told me his secret. So I should tell him mine. I keep my voice even. Matter-of-fact. Not panicky. "My dad left. A couple of weeks before Christmas." Nine weeks and five days, counting yesterday and today.

"What do you mean, left? He disappeared?"

I nod. "Supposedly he went to Mexico to take care of my great grandmother. But we haven't heard from him. I don't even think he knows where we moved to."

"Why don't you write to him?"

"I've never met my bisabuelita, or been to her house. We don't know her address."

"Oh," says River, and he stands up. "Hey, I got to go. When you get out, come over. We'll find your dad on my computer. I'm a good detective. Cross my finger!" And he wraps his thumb around his finger and grins at me. He opens the door and says, "Live long and prosper," holding up his hand.

I wave back. My heart feels the same as River's hand. Missing things. Doing the best it can. But then I see his drawing of me. Standing there, looking out at the beautiful apartments I imagined. And I feel something very little plant itself in my heart. A little seed, a *pepita* of hope. I cross my fingers, on both hands, and make two wishes.

CHAPTER SEVEN

D IS FOR DIABETES

I just want to tell you, don't go wishing for diabetes. It's not a great way to get a week off school. Me and Mr. Hawaii spent a lot of quality time together while I was in the hospital. Now Mami won't let me leave the apartment, so me and Mr. TV are spending time until I go back to school tomorrow. I wonder if Mr. RF, Robert Frost, missed me. Or anybody. Not that I care.

I'm getting pretty good at checking my levels with my very own lancing device and glucometer. I'm not quite as good at giving myself an insulin shot. Mostly Mami has to do it. In my belly, or my arm, or my leg, but not the same place twice in a row. All this for a person who hates needles.

But guess what's the hardest? Balancing my diet. Fruit is good. But don't choose bananas. Berries are the best. And expensive. Meat? Great. Eggs? Great. But be careful about adding tortillas and rice.

"Portion control," the nutritionist told Mami.

"Self-control," Mami told me.

"Out of control," I told her. "That's what this is."

Before diabetes I ate Pop-Tarts, doughnuts, or Cinnamon Toast Crunch for breakfast, or nothing at all if I ran out of time. Guess what? Those are not good choices. I have a list of good choices now:

1) Peanut-butter-and-apple sandwich

2) Tortilla stuffed with scrambled eggs

3) Cheerios with strawberries

These are great choices if you happen to have an apple lying around. Or time to scramble eggs. And if you think strawberries last more than two seconds in our fridge before Danny or Danita pop them like candy, you're wrong.

On the first day I came home from the hospital everybody acted so nice. I got a little bag from Danny and Danita. Bubble bath. Body wash. And my own perfume called Happy.

"So you can stop borrowing mine," said Danny.

"Very funny," I said.

Danita fixed my hair and painted my nails.

"So you can start looking like the diva you are," said Danita.

"Very funny," I said.

The next day Danita and Andrea walked to Robert Frost to get my homework.

"Your teacher is intense," Andrea told me. "Look at all this work."

"I can't believe you told her you didn't speak Spanish," Danita told me. "You're such a brat."

"This is messy. Messy work," said Mami when she saw my take-home folder with the graded papers in it. "You can do better."

And everybody went back to acting normal.

Mami and Danny rearranged their work schedules. Just until I go back to school. So, except for about an hour every afternoon, one of them stays home with me during the day.

When Mami leaves me alone on the first day, I get my skateboard out of the closet and start practicing my bling for Spring Fling. I can already hear Yari say, "Wow, DeeDee, I can't believe you skateboard." First I work on getting on and balancing. I'm a "regular" stance so I put my left foot on first. I practice a little trick Freddie taught me: upside down board, toe under, flip and jump. It's pretty tricky, but not a real trick.

The second day I take my skateboard into the hall-way. Did you know that skateboarding on carpet is practically impossible? No matter how hard you push, the skateboard barely rolls. But it's great for working on flip tricks or flipping people over. Poor Mrs. Robinson, one of my new neighbors, found that out when she opened her door. She landed, kersplat, on her you-know-what, and spilled her coffee. It's easy to find my apartment door now. The one after the monster coffee stain.

The day before I go back to school, I take my skate-board out to the slushy parking lot. Why do they need these speed bumps? As if someone is going to go 90 miles an hour in and out of my parking lot. I go back upstairs with wet knees and a scraped elbow. And when Mami comes home, suddenly I have skateboarding rules.

•

Mami walks me to Robert Frost on my first day back. River waves at us as his yellow bus turns the corner. It seems like forever since he visited me in the hospital. I haven't seen him from my balcony and I feel awk-ward knocking on his door. I mean, what would I say? Hi, remember me? The diabetic who knocked you over and then insulted your deaf school? He's probably for-gotten that he promised to help me find Papi. Besides, Mami told Danita a thousand times that I'm supposed to rest when I get home from school.

Mami has forms for the nurse, Mrs. Marsh, whose room is right across from the office. I see a poster on the wall—THE SEVEN B'S TO COME SEE ME: BLEEDING. BAD BREATHING. BROKEN. BARFING. BURNING UP. BEE STING. BIG BUMP. Hmph. I guess I don't have to come. Diabetes starts with a D. By The Way. And it's not on the list.

Mami talks to Mrs. Marsh, doing the best she can to explain things without anybody translating. I sit on the paper-coated couch-bed and feel silly. Mrs. Marsh pats Mami's hand.

"Don't worry. We'll take good care of Dinora for you," she says.

Mami kisses me and I'm glad nobody sees. "*Te portas bien*," she says.

Mrs. Marsh shows me where to put my kit of diabetes supplies. She checks my levels and tut-tuts.

"And what did we eat for breakfast?" she asks.

"I don't know what you ate, but I ate Cinnamon Toast Crunch," I say.

She laughs and says, "Oatmeal with blueberries. And they had doughnuts in the teacher's lounge. I can't resist doughnuts when they call my name."

"I can't resist Pop-Tarts when they jump into my mouth," I say.

"Ah-ha," says Mrs. Marsh. "So we both need to resist temptation, don't we?"

When I walk into class everybody acts like they're my long lost best friends asking me questions and volunteering to help me. Except for Noodlenose. She says nothing.

Apparently Mrs. Cruella knows all about my diabetes, because ten minutes before lunch and recess, she tells me it's time to visit the nurse. "Who would like to accompany DeeDee to Mrs. Marsh?" she asks. A whole bunch of hands hit the air. Not Noodlenose's, of course. She makes a sour-pickle face. Mrs. Marsh calls on Nicole and we walk out the door together. On the way Nicole asks me questions about diabetes. When I poke my finger she says, "Ooh, you must be so brave. I could never do that."

Mrs. Marsh tells Nicole to wait in the hall while she gives me my insulin shot. She looks at my glucose reading and together we create my lunch menu—chicken patty on a bun, one orange, one bag of cucumber slices, and plain milk.

"I can't believe you have to have a shot every day," says Nicole. "Does it hurt?"

"You get used to it," I say, like an old pro.

When we get to the lunchroom there's a problem. No oranges. Bananas instead. No chicken patties. Ham and cheese instead. Bull-face, the lunch supervisor, calls Mrs. Marsh on the intercom, and in front of the entire lunchroom they figure out how to substitute. I mean, really? I may as well just bring my lunch.

Samantha squishes over so there's space for me and Nicole. I notice an assortment of pink and purple colors on all the girls' shiny nails Only Nancy's nails are blue. I guess I missed the mani-pedi birthday party. Danita polished my nails, but it's already chipping off. I put one hand in my lap, the other with my fingers curled under my sandwich. It's not like I would have even been invited anyway.

"Hey," says Samantha. "You got your nails done, too."

Fudge buckets. She noticed. "Yah," I say. "My sister."

"Too bad you were in the hospital. Nancy's mom got us all mani-pedis at her salon."

Nancy looks up, her eyes very frosty. "Yes. Too bad," she says. "But maybe Sherie will invite you to her slumber party, right Sherie?"

Sherie gives Nancy a jab with her elbow. "Oh, for sure. I don't know how many people I'm allowed to have, but I'll ask."

She's probably lying, but still, even thinking about being invited makes me hopeful. That *pepita* growing a little. "Thanks," I say.

Hannah shouts at me from the end of the table. "Hey DeeDee, can I take you to the nurse after lunch?"

"Sure," I shout back, and smile.

During reading group time, I head to see Yari. "DeeDee!" she says, excited to see me. "Mrs. Krewell told me you were in the hospital."

"Yah. I needed a little vacation from school," I say,

Yari laughs a good belly laugh. I really like people who do that. "Let's get started," she says. Then she says, "I'm going to catch you up," sounding just like Mr. Hawaii.

•

When I visit Mrs. Marsh before lunch the next day, she makes me open my lunch box.

"Happy Groundhog's Day," she says. "Good choice." She points to my tortilla spread with peanut butter. "But what are these?" She holds up my red apple and my bag of Doritos.

"Apples are healthy." Danny's mentor gave him that apple and he gave it to me.

"The size of the apple matters. And look at the label on these Doritos," says Mrs. Marsh.

"When are you going to put me on the Seven B's? I come here every day. I should be on the poster."

Mrs. Marsh laughs. "You don't start with B, and neither does diabetes."

"We could start a new poster. The Seven D's. DeeDee, diet, diabetes, Doritos . . ."

"Eat half of this apple. And half of these chips. And no Sprite. Get a milk from the cart."

Later, in P.E., Mr. Incredible sends everyone to their fitness stations except me. He walks up to me and I smell hamburgers. Burger King, maybe.

"I didn't know you had diabetes. If you have a health issue I'm supposed to be notified."

"I just found out," I say.

"Well, next time, tell me right away. You can sit over there until we're done with physical fitness testing." He points to a bench where Nicole is reading a book.

"Why are you here?" I ask her when I sit down.

"Forgot my gym shoes," she says. We sit there like two bumps. I don't understand why I can't do physical fitness testing. Do people with diabetes have to sit around all the time? Dr. Zebra-Face didn't warn me about that. And if I have to sit around all the time, what about Spring Fling? What about skateboarding? What about dancing?

When I get home from school, Danita and Andrea—yes, she's always at our apartment—have a snack ready. Some sort of brown paste that looks like baby poop, and celery sticks.

"What is it?" I ask.

"Hummus," says Andrea. "It's good for you."

"No thank you," I say.

"Try it," says Danita. "It's made out of garbanzo beans, the same beans Mami puts in pozole."

I take a teensy taste. "I don't like it."

"Then just eat the celery," says Danita. She and Andrea go off to her bedroom with a *Quinceañera* magazine. I switch the TV to my saved episodes of *Dancing with the Stars*. I hear giggling and rustling so I tiptoe close to the door and open it a crack. Sure enough, they're sharing a bag of Doritos—the green bag—Dinamita Chile Limón. I dump the hummus—hum-ugh I call it, into the sink and put on some of the Passion-Pink lip gloss Danita dropped at the hospital, then twirl and slide right along with Jordan Fisher and Lindsay Arnold.

Me and Papi watch all the TV competitions together. *Dancing with the Stars. The Voice. America's Got Talent. American Idol.* "Let's sign you up, Gordita," he used to say. "I'll be your agent." Everybody clapped when he and I danced at Tía Karina's wedding last year. Is he watching our shows now, without me? Is he dancing with another little girl? I pour myself a bowl of Cinnamon Toast Crunch and start my homework.

And you know? It seems easier. Maybe I'm paying better attention because I'm not half asleep all the time. Or maybe working with Yari is helping.

At bedtime, Mami strokes my head. "So much good for you."

She means it's good I have no more accidents. And that is good news, isn't it? Just in case Sherie invites me to her sleepover.

Late at night, Danny comes home. No more wrapping-paper sounds when he sits down on the couch by me because I don't need the plastic tablecloth anymore.

"So, how's things at NGYCP?" I ask.

"I might be able to take my GED soon," he says.

"GED?"

"General Equivalency Diploma—like a high school diploma. You can't get into the army without it."

"Oh," I say. But if Danny gets in the army, he'll go away again, won't he?

"How's Frosty going?" he asks, squeezing my toes.

We both use Yari's name for RF now. "Okay," I say. "Everybody's been really nice."

"Been to see River?" Danny asks.

"Not yet," I say. "Mami wants me to rest after school." She always says don't play rough. Dr. Zebra-Face told her diabetics can bruise easily and heal slowly.

"I shot some baskets with him while you were in the hospital. He's pretty funny."

Hmm. Danny and River shot baskets? I have a funny little hiccup in my stomach. But why should that bother me? I barely even know River.

•

We're done with poetry now so on Thursday we start figurative language.

Mrs. Cruella assigns each group a new chart. We're illustrating similes, which if you don't know, compares one thing to another thing. Kind of like Mrs. Cruella compared to Cruella DeVille or Nancy to a noodle nose. Or people in my group who stink like farts.

While Mrs. Cruella makes her rounds I zip to the bathroom. I don't have to get permission anymore because of diabetes. Isn't that a bonus? When I return I see Mrs. Cruella talking to my group. She has her hands on her hips, which isn't a good sign. I walk up behind her and hear Nancy say, "Our group works really well together." When Mrs. Cruella walks away Nancy rolls her eyes.

I sit down at the table and Nicole says, "I love your idea of people being as frosty as Elsa's castle, DeeDee. So creative."

"And we can put the fluffy-as-snow clouds around the castle with the diamond stars in the sky," says Samantha.

Nancy doesn't say anything and that's weird, isn't it? And Sherie shares her markers. Also weird.

My levels are way off when I stop to see Mrs. Marsh and she grumbles at me. "DeeDee, do you want to end up in the hospital again? What did you eat for breakfast?"

Oh My Gatos. The glucometer doesn't lie, even if I do. Even if I forgot to mention that I had an extra Pop-Tart this morning and a few M&M's. It makes me mad that people who don't have to use a glucometer get to lie all the time. If that spot-disappearing spray doesn't work out, I think I'll invent a truthometer.

During lunch kids from the Student Leadership Team walk around to each lunch table and remind everyone about the Spring Fling. Yari and a kind-of-cute boy come to our table with sign-up forms.

She smiles when she sees me. "DeeDee, *qué te pasa, calabaza?*"

I giggle. "*Nada, nada, limonada,*" forgetting about speaking Spanish.

She hands me a few forms. "Here pass these out to your friends," she says. "And I better see you at the tryouts!"

When they're gone, Sherie whispers, "Ooh, Brandon is so cute."

"Who's signing up for Spring Fling?" I ask.

"Can you be in it with diabetes?" asks Samantha.

"My aunt has diabetes and she has to be really careful about her activity levels, or she gets hypoglycemia," says Noodlenose Nancy. "Plus, she's fat. Fat people get diabetes."

"Is diabetes catching?" asks Despicable Me Sherie.

"I don't know, is being annoying catching?" I ask. I grab my lunch garbage, leave the forms on the table, and head to the bathroom.

Once I get into the bathroom stall, I try not to cry. Maybe Despicable Me Sherie didn't mean anything. I mean, I had the same questions when Dr. Zebra-Face first told me. And Nancy doesn't matter. No, she does not. Samantha and Nicole and Colin have been nice. And Yari says, starting a new school is like biting into a burrito in the middle. Ha! That's a pretty good simile. I have a checkup with Dr. Zebra-Face today. And I hope she's ready for a ton of questions.

I run to catch up as my class leaves the lunchroom, and I slide into line just in time to hear Samantha say, "We're supposed to be nice to her, Sherie. Mrs. Cruella told us we had to."

"I feel sorry for her, don't you?" says Nicole.

"Oh, yah. Poor little DeeDee," says Noodlenose Nancy.

"You mean poor little PeePee," says Despicable Me Sherie, and they all laugh.

I slink back to the end of the line. Something in my chest squeezes so hard I can't breathe. I scrunch down into my jacket. Fakers. They're all fakers. Wolves, like Papi told Danny. I hate Robert Frost Elementary.

While Mrs. Cruella works with a group, I find my assigned computer in the numbered slot on the cart. A little gold heart charm is caught between the slot and the edge of the cart door, so I pluck it out and put it in my pocket. Finders keepers. I walk back along the windows to my desk. Suddenly Sherie raises her hand and waves it like she's drying her armpits. Before Mrs. Cruella even calls on her she wails. "My heart. My heart. I lost my heart."

Nancy butts in. "She means her heart charm, Mrs. Krewell."

I close my hand around the pebble-small heart charm in my pocket while my own heart feels rock-heavy.

CHAPTER SEVEN

D IS FOR DETECTIVE

River's bus pulls into the parking lot as I'm crossing the street. I see him jump out and run into our building. Is he a faker friend, too? Mrs. Cruella gave me a note from the office just before dismissal. My appointment is delayed so Mami will meet me at home and not the bus stop. But Danita won't be home to watch me. She and Andrea made big plans when they found out they didn't have to "babysit" for me.

I let myself in with the key Mami makes me put in my backpack every morning and hang it back on the hook next to the door. Danita must have left her alarm clock on this morning—music is blaring from her room. I sink onto the couch. I really do wish I could go back in time to Lincoln Elementary. I would do a much better job of being friends with everybody. Even annoying Abiola.

When I go to the bathroom I see Danita's door standing open a crack, and I'm tempted to go in and turn off her alarm clock radio. But even if I don't touch anything she always knows when I've been in her room. Then I hear something else. Gulpy breaths and squeaky sobs. I put my eye right up to the crack. Danita sits on the floor holding a picture in her lap—the photo of Papi that Mami keeps on the end table. She's bawling. And I mean bawling.

"It's all ruined, Papi. And it's all your fault. DeeDee's sick. Mami's tired. Danny's joining the army. And my *quinceañera*. The father-daughter dance. Who will do the first dance with me, now?"

I back away. I'm stunned. Bossy Danita, the Queen Bee, crying? My stomach tightens. I never thought about Danita missing Papi. But it's not his fault, is it? It's our fault. We didn't want to go with him. We weren't good enough.

Then I think: But what if it's nobody's fault? What if he's hurt somewhere? Kidnapped? It can happen. Me and Mr. TV saw plenty of shows about kidnapping.

I need to find Papi. That's the only way we will know for sure. I need a detective.

River. I need to visit River.

I write Mami a quick note—I'M AT APART-MENT #311—and grab the key I hung by the door.

I hesitate before knocking. It's bad to say, but when I think about his distinctions, his electro-pology—electro-dactpoly—oh fudge buckets, his fingers, I get a shiver. But I don't want to be like Noodlenose Nancy and Despicable Me Sherie. I tell myself I'm not going to let a little thing like Bluetooth ears and Star Trek fingers get in my way.

River opens the door before I knock. "I saw you walking over" he says.

Which makes me wonder if every day since I came home from the hospital, he's been watching and waiting for me.

"Sparkling water? Raspberry or passion fruit?" he asks.

He talks fast and as if he's got cotton padding on his tongue. "I can't . . ." I start to say.

"I know. I researched. This is flavored water with sparkles, you know, carbonation. No sugar or sodium."

Who is this kid? I think. "Raspberry."

I look around. The walls are covered with artwork. Covered. All over the hall, kitchen, living room. Paintings, drawings, paper collages. Faces. Planets. Dinosaurs. Sunsets. The colors are amazing. "Who . . .?" I start to ask.

"Me. Art therapy. Since I was two." His two-finger hand points around the room. "I do that Young Rembrandts program at the park district. You should sign up."

Oh, sure. I think. We've got lots of leftover money for that.

"Where—" I start to ask, but River opens the front closet, takes my coat, and hangs it up.

"How—" I start, but River jumps in again.

"I played basketball with your brother. He's nice."

"Are you—"

"Nah, I don't really play. I do play soccer."

"That's not what I was going to ask."

River zips into the kitchen and brings me my sparkling water. "What were you going to ask?"

I turn to make sure he can see my lips. "If you are ever going to let me finish a sentence."

He looks embarrassed. "Sorry. It's just . . . I mean . . . I don't . . . you know. I told you I go to school with a lot of little kids."

River puts his sparkling water on the end table next to the couch. A jar of markers sits between two laptop computers on the coffee table.

I have no idea what to say. It's awkward.

"So—" we both start to say at the same time.

"You go," I say.

"Have you been back to the hospital for a follow-up?"

"I have an appointment today."

"I read it's hard at first to get your levels stable."

"Oh," I say.

"And I read, too, that if you're really active, like dance or something, it might lower your glucose levels."

"Oh," I say again.

"And the body uses insulin more efficiently if you dance regularly, so you might need less insulin." River beams at me. "See, you'll live long and prosper."

He's such a geek. And it's like he read my mind again. Has he been spying on me? Why would he say dance?

"Okay, don't be mad at me. Danny told me you like to dance, and I thought . . . well . . . it's just that . . . I don't usually have anybody to compete with me on Dance Forever."

Oh Land O'Lakes. "You have Dance Forever? I love Dance Forever! Are you any good?"

And he is. Because after a half hour, I can't come close to his score. He's better than me. And I'm pretty good. If I decide to go to Danita's *quinceañera* I should ask Danita to invite him. Then I'd for sure have a decent dance partner and not some dorky cousin.

A video starts in my head. Me dancing a ballad with Danita's *damas*, girl attendants. River dancing with the *chambelanes*, boy attendants. Then Danita's court separating, grabbing the hands of the boys and weaving between them. When they come to River, he holds out his hand and . . . the video dissolves. I shudder. They might not want to hold River's hand. Because of his distinction. Oh My Gatos. How embarrassing! I feel the color creep up to my face.

And then I'm ashamed. What about River? How would he feel? So hurt. So rejected. Exactly how I feel every day at Robert Frost. It must be the same for River. Is that why he visited me in the hospital?

"Your turn," River says, out of breath.

I jump back onto the mat. Well, I don't have to worry about a stupid *quinceañera*, because I'm not going anyway.

River's mom comes into the room while we're resting from dancing a tiebreaker. River introduces me. "Mom, DeeDee. DeeDee, Mrs. Ramos-Henry."

"Oh, DeeDee, I'm so happy to meet you."

She shakes my hand. As if I'm so famous that she's lucky to meet me. She's beautiful, and I don't say that about too many people. Her black-as-the-night, wavy hair brushes the table as she leans to kiss the top of River's head. I smell flowers. She wears skinny Wild-Blue-Yonder jeans and a long, flowing, gauzy Cerise shirt.

I look at her hands. They're perfect. All her fingers right where they're supposed to be. No electro-whatever.

When she goes into the kitchen, River whispers, "It's okay. I told her about you and your dad."

"What'd you do that for?"

"I need her password if you want me to look stuff up." He switches on the laptop. "She's a paralegal. That's an assistant to a lawyer."

"I know what a paralegal is." That's a lie, but I don't like being so ignorant compared to River. "What does your dad do?"

"He died in the army when I was three." River's rolls his hands together like he did in the hospital.

"Oh, that's too bad."

"I know. I hardly remember him." He keeps rolling his hands. He doesn't look at me. Then he starts clicking away on the computer, keeping his voice low. "My mom tells me about him, but it's not the same."

"I wish my mom talked about my dad, but nobody talks about him. I'm starting to forget." This scares me. It scares me so much. Maybe it's the same for River. Maybe that's why he wants to help me find my dad.

"What's his name?" asks River.

"Daniel Diaz, the same as my brother."

"Birth date?" he asks.

"Um, I think September 17th."

"Year?"

"I don't know." Are kids supposed to know what year their parents are born?

River stops typing. "There are over a hundred people named Daniel Diaz."

"Oh," I say.

"Don't worry, we can figure it out." He gets up. "I'm getting a piece of string cheese. Want one?"

"Okay," I say.

He comes back with a bowl of strawberries and two sticks of string cheese.

"What kind of lunches does Robert Frost have?" he asks.

"Boring. I have to plan my lunch with the nurse so I'm not overdoing the carbs."

River takes a long string off the cheese stick and eats it like a noodle.

"Look." He points to the laptop. "Some of these people might not even be real. They could be fake accounts, like fake news." He closes the laptop. "But the real news is I'm for sure transferring to a new school. Either Maya Angelou because they already have some hard-of-hearing students, or Robert Frost because I can walk there."

"Oh," I say. "Well, Robert Frost takes some getting used to. I'm pretty much a straight-A student, so I can handle it. But I think my teacher hates Mexicans. She thinks bilingual kids can't read." I finish my string cheese and bite into a strawberry.

"What school did you go to before?" River asks.

"Lincoln Elementary. All my friends were super sad when I moved, but I've already got lots of new friends."

A knock interrupts us. "DeeDee, *ven, nos vamos.*" It's Mami, telling me it's time to go.

I walk to the closet to get my coat. Jutting out behind the coats I see a wheel. I pull the coats to the side and see the deck of a skateboard. "What's this?"

"My skateboard," says River.

"I have one, too," I say. "I've been skating for a couple of years. Danny's friend Freddie taught me."

"I'm not that good," says River. "I can carve a bit and get some air. Maybe when it's warm we could go to the skatepark and you could teach me some tricks."

"Yah. Great," I say, thinking how stupid I am for lying about skating because now I can't go to the skatepark until I'm better at skating.

I open the door and River holds up his hand. "Live long and prosper," he says.

"Same to you," I say.

Me and Mami head down the hall. We've just passed our apartment when River leans his head out in the hall. "Hey, DeeDee. Can you teach me that trick?" He points at the carpet and I look down. I'm standing in front of Mrs. Robinson's door. Right on the big monster stain.

I whip around. He's making fun of me. He's just like everybody else. He knew the whole time I'm a lousy skater. But instead of a nasty, know-it-all look on his face, he's grinning. "Don't worry," he calls after me. "I'll teach you the trick of not falling down."

•

I find myself thinking about River during school the next day. Not in a mushy-boyfriend way, but an I-had-fun-at-his-house way. A *pepita*-of-hope-sprouting-little-leaves way.

But then I think, what will happen if he does go to Robert Frost? Will he expect me to be his helper friend? I'm not sure I can handle more teasing from Nancy and Sherie. I know that's selfish. But River won't be happy at Robert Frost. He already told me that I wouldn't be happy at his school. I cross my fingers that he goes to Maya Angelou.

Yari's back in peer-tutoring business and she saved her lunch carrots for me, so we nibble while she tutors me.

"Are you going to try out for Spring Fling?" she asks.

"I might. What do you think about skateboarding?"

"Oh-Em-Gee. That is so sick. We've never had anybody skateboard. Wait until I tell the Student Leadership Team," she says, twirling her string bracelet.

We're working on the difference between a character's feelings and a character's traits.

"You know," says Yari, showing me a chart. "These emoticons with the labels are a nice way to figure out feelings in general." She points at nervous. "I'm always nervous around boys." Then she points at frustrated. "And I get so frustrated about the way people treat Latinas."

I point at discouraged. "I wish there was an emoticon for feeling stupid."

"No you don't," says Yari and points at the proud emoticon. "You've made lots of progress. My teacher says instead of a fixed mindset, we should use a growth mindset. So instead of saying I'm stupid, you say I need new strategies. Instead of saying this is too hard for me, say I can do this with effort and work."

"But I have diabetes, so things are hard for me," I say.

"Nope," says Yari. "You just need new strategies. And—a new purple shirt."

She pulls a shirt from her backpack. "It's a little too short for me, but it's from my favorite store where I get most of my clothes, Sun and Stars Boutique."

"Oh My Gatos," I say. "Thanks." Maybe next week I will invite Yari to come over. Maybe Mami will make flan. Yari loves flan but her mom barely cooks because of her job.

When the bell rings at the end of the day, Mrs. Cruella dismisses the class by calling out the names of the students with all completed assignments. I hear Nancy whisper, "See you tonight," to Sherie after her name is called. So tonight's the sleepover, and my invitation must have gotten lost. Well la-di-da.

"DeeDee, I'm missing three assignments from you," says Mrs. Cruella. "Three."

I dig in my desk and come up with two half-finished language arts papers. I zip to the hall, dig in my backpack, and come up with one half-finished math paper. I smooth out the wrinkles and place all three on Mrs. Cruella's desk.

"Hmm," says Mrs. Cruella. "It appears these haven't been completed. Under the circumstances, I will give you full credit if they're completed and on my desk tomorrow."

So, thanks to Mrs. Cruella, it's later than usual when I walk across our speed-bump parking lot. I hear a basketball bouncing and see River and Danny on the court, playing. I run up the stairs two at a time.

"You're late," says Danita. "Your little friend came looking for you."

I throw my backpack on the couch, go to the bathroom, and start for the door.

"Not until you have a snack," says Danita. "Mami says."

I wolf down crackers and cheese, then run out the door. Danny comes toward me, bouncing the ball.

"Gordita," he says. "How was school?"

"Where's River?" I ask, looking around.

"I don't know. He went to a friend's house, I think."

Something between my throat and my stomach squeezes. I see the emoticon faces on the chart Yari and I worked with today. What am I feeling? Disappointment? Loneliness? No. I realize with a start, I'm jealous. Jealous of River and Danny. Jealous of River and his friend. Jealous they're having fun without me. Really? What is my problem? He's just my Star Trek weirdo neighbor.

"He was looking for you," says Danny. "I think he wanted to tell you he's starting at Frosty on Monday."

River's transferring to Robert Frost? You know that feeling when you're in the first roller coaster car at the very top of the drop off? That's how my stomach feels right now. What will it be like with River at my school? Will he embarrass me? Why do these things happen to me?

"Here, take the ball up, will you? I have to go to work."

I march upstairs. Danita's pink overnight bag sits on the couch. "Where are you going?"

"Andrea's house. When Mami gets home," she says.

If I had a bedroom I'd huff right in and slam the door. Who needs sleepovers? Who needs friends? Not me. Me and my angry emoticon face can have fun all by ourselves.

CHAPTER EIGHT

D IS FOR DETECTIVE (FOR REAL THIS TIME)

On Saturday morning after Mami goes to work, I'm still jealous River went to his friend's house yesterday. And I know I'm being ridiculous. It's not like he has to wait around for me. I almost talk myself out of going to his house, but I remember Yari's pep talk. I need new strategies. I can do this. As soon as Danita comes straggling home from her sleepover, with Andrea following her, I grab the key from the hook and march down the hall. I knock and wait. And wait. I knock again. And wait and wait. Maybe everyone in the world except DeeDee Diaz is at a sleepover. I knock one more time and turn to leave.

The door flies open. "I didn't hear you knock," River says. "My implant batteries were charging."

"Oh," I say. "Danny said you were at a friend's yesterday. I thought maybe it was a sleepover."

River looks puzzled. "I had to go with my mom to work last night. Shondrea, my babysitter, got sick."

That spot between my throat and my stomach pitter-patters. Stop doing that, I tell it.

"We can work here," he says, pointing at the two computers. "After you left on Thursday, I bookmarked sites for locating missing persons. But it will really help if you can find his birth certificate or his driver's license or something."

"Where would I find those?" I watch as he pulls up a list of websites from a folder marked MISSING FATHER, using his thumbs and four fingers on the keyboard. He's fast. Way faster than I am at typing.

I stare at the markers on the coffee table. STAEDTLER art markers. I pick them up one by one. Bordeaux 23. Ultramarine Blue 37. Turquoise 54. Violet 6. Mauve 260. What's the point of having a number and a name? Unless it's a way to keep track of them..

"Is Mauve the last color?" I ask.

"Why?"

"Because it's the highest number I see. "

"I don't know. I only have the set of forty-eight."

"Well, that's dumb—I mean stupid," I say.

"True. Speaking of numbers, what about doing a little detective work? Is there a wallet or a stack of bills in your mom's room you can look through?" He juts his pointy chin toward my apartment.

"Maybe." I'm a little doubtful. "Now?"

"I'll leave the door open for you. Think like a detective." He says this in a mysterious voice, one thick eyebrow arching up over his wide, brown eyes.

Weirdo, I think.

As soon as I walk into the hall, a lump of worry forms in between my throat and my lungs. What if we actually find my dad and he doesn't want to come home? What if he's in some kind of trouble? If Mami knew something, wouldn't she have told us? Maybe I shouldn't go snooping around in her private stuff.

I open the door. Danita and Andrea are eating Oreos and watching a soap opera. I have no idea how Danita stays so skinny when all she does is eat.

"I thought you were going to your friend's house," she says.

"I am. I just need something."

It must be a good episode. They don't even turn their heads. I casually walk down the hall. Think like a detective. I sneak into Mami's room and open her top drawer.

There, on top of her flowered pajamas, Papi's face stares up at me. He's so young. His arm around Mami in her white dress. Their wedding picture. I didn't know she saved it from the fire. I take a good look. They seem so happy. Maybe he left because having kids ruined their life.

I turn the frame over and see a little card with names and dates and some numbers stuck under the edge.

"What are you doing, DeeDee?" Danita calls.

"Nothing," I yell. I slide the picture under my shirt. Right near where the lump is making it hard to breathe. I already feel guilty.

I shuffle around under the clothes and find a twenty-dollar bill. For just one minute I think like a thief and not a detective. Into my front pocket goes the twenty.

I flip through the stack of envelopes on the top of the dresser. CHASE BANK. SIMMONS PROPERTY MANAGEMENT. NATIONAL GUARD YOUTH CHALLENGE PROGRAM. US DEPARTMENT OF HOMELAND SECURITY. US Department of Homeland Security? I grab the envelope.

On the bottom shelf of the nightstand I see a fat brown folder. I flop it open on the bed. Medical bills. My medical bills. I study the one on top. It's got Papi's name and insurance listed, but it says CLAIM DENIED, whatever that means. I fold the medical bill up small and stuff it in my back pocket. A nagging, bothersome idea keeps poking into my brain.

What does Mami know? And why doesn't she want to talk about it? If she told us what's going on, then I wouldn't have to sneak around, would I? It's her fault I'm acting this way. Her fault. Her fault Papi went away without us. Because she didn't want to go.

"DeeDee!" Danita blasts the door open, scaring me to death.

"What?" I jerk the folder shut.

"What are you doing in here?"

"Nothing." I march past Queen Bee. "Does mom know you eat junk food in front of me?"

"We thought you were at your little friend's house," says Andrea.

"I guess we're even then." I don't say goodbye. I hate being the little sister.

The walk next door to River's takes me a long time. I almost go back in a panic and put everything away. I think about telling River I couldn't find anything to help us. But then I put my teeth together and bust back into River's house.

"Wow! Good work," he says when I show him the picture with the card on the back, the Homeland Security envelope, and the medical bill. The twenty dollars stays in my pocket. "Your dad's handsome. You kind of look like him."

I don't say thank you, but I think it's a compliment.

River studies the medical bill. "Claims can be denied for lots of reasons. Something your insurance doesn't cover. Or it's possible your dad's insurance ended because he doesn't work there any more."

"You mean he got fired and that's why he left?"

"Or he couldn't get time off to visit your . . ." River stops.

"Bisabuelita," I say.

"Bisabuelita. And they fired him because he left."

When he takes the US Department of Homeland Security envelope from me, my hand shakes. I'm scared to see what's inside.

"Hmm," says River. "It's a legal notice from the US Citizenship and Immigration Services. It says that your dad is in violation for not appearing before a judge in December."

"What does that mean?"

"I don't know for sure. Does your dad have a green card? Or is he undocumented?"

"No," I say loudly. "He's not undocumented. He's been here forever. He works at TAICO. " Papi's had the same job for as long as I can remember. He talks about which president he wants to vote for. He's got a driver's license. There's no way he's undocumented.

"I'm just asking but that's another good idea. We can call his work and see if he's left a forwarding address."

All the time we've been talking, River's been typing stuff into the computer. I'm fascinated that he can talk and type at the same time. "Okay, I think I found something." He points to a map on his computer screen.

"His name and birth date on the card show his birthplace as here." He points to Tixtla de Guerrero, Mexico.

"But there's addresses from a few years ago near here." He points to Guadalajara, Jalisco. "And here and here." He points to Ciudad Juárez and Piedras Negras.

"Sound familiar?"

I squint at the map and sound out the names the best I can. "Maybe. But I've never been to Mexico. And I don't remember Papi or Mami ever going there, either," I say, scanning the map. "But these two towns are close to the border, so maybe he went there, at least first, since Guadalajara is really far away."

"Okay. Don't freak out, but . . . since he didn't contact you, he might be in a hospital. So let's search for all the hospitals between those last two places and the border, and add their addresses to the spreadsheet. It's saved there, in the corner. And if he doesn't have a place to stay, he might be at a shelter or a church. I'll do those."

"Addresses? Are we going to send letters to them? How are we going to afford to buy all those stamps? They don't even know us. They're not just going to tell us where my dad is."

"Email addresses. Mostly. A maybe a few snail-mail letters. And no, they might not tell us, but we can ask them to have him contact us, can't we? Oh, also, put anything you can about your dad in the missing person form I downloaded from the National Missing and Unidentified Persons System. If you don't know something leave it blank." He points to the saved document on the desktop of the laptop I'm using.

This guy is smart. Way smart. I get started. First I fill out the form. At least, I try. But I don't know all the information and I have to subtract for how old he is and I'm not sure about how to spell his relative's names.

Then I start on the hospitals. River's church and shelter list is three times as long as mine in just a few minutes. An hour goes by. River talks about stuff. His favorite colors and animals. How he won first place in an art show one time. How he wants to be in the army like his dad, but he can't because of his ears.

"I thought you said your electro-thing was inherited. But your mom doesn't have it," I blurt out and point at his hands. I can't keep the question inside any longer.

"Ectrodactyly? It is. From my dad. But he didn't really know because his little fingers were just shaped weird." He puts the cursor over a spot on the desktop and clicks. A picture of a good-looking army man fills the screen. A very good-looking black army man. Which

I guess explains why River's skin is a different color from his mom's. I'm a different color from Mami, too. She's sandy brown and I'm deck brown. The color of the deck in front of our old trailer. *Morena*, Mami would say. "Stay out of the sun, *mi morenita*," Mami always tells me.

"Oh. Were your parents shocked—I mean surprised—when you came out like that? I mean, when they saw your ectrodactyly?" Fudge buckets. Why can't I remember my manners until it's too late?

River stares at me. "Were your parents shocked—I mean surprised—about your diabetes?" His voice is sharp and mocking.

"I'm sorry. I just wondered. I didn't mean to be rude."

"It's okay. Lots of people are rude. But I want you to understand how it sounds when you ask things like that, because you're not in the rude category."

I feel better. River sees me as better than I am. I don't want to be in the rude category, like Nancy and Sherie, but sometimes I am.

River goes on, "I'm sure my parents were shocked. I mean, what's the first thing a parent checks for? Ten fingers and ten toes. People still get shocked, and it's frustrating. But nobody's perfect, are they?" He keeps rubbing his hands, over and around each other, like he did at the hospital. It must be a nervous habit.

"People say such stupid things to me. Usually, I don't say anything, even if I want to." He gives an evil chuckle. "But one time I said, 'You're so perfect on the outside, you must be really messed up on the inside,' and I just walked away."

"Whoa, that's good." I think for a second. That's also true. Everybody is messed up. Outside and inside. I have diabetes. Danny's hair sticks up in the back and he dropped out of high school. Danita has one foot that's a half-size bigger than the other and is a huge brat. Andrea is supposed to wear glasses but is too vain.

I say, "It doesn't seem fair. Some people's defects are tiny."

"Yah. It's not fair. But what can people do about it? My mom tells me I have to rise to the challenge. And remember, they're distinctions, not defects."

I lean back on the couch and sigh. "Diabetes still feels like a defect to me."

"Want to take a break? Go get your board," he says.

"I'm not allowed to practice in the parking lot anymore."

"The slush melted on the sidewalk."

"But the sign says no skateboarding."

"We know the manager. It's okay when nobody's out there."

I run to grab my board and, yes, my helmet and pads, and we skitter down the stairs. River coaches me on my foot placement, which gives me better balance, and I skate way better than I ever did at the trailer park. River shows me how to ollie. That's when you have both feet on the board and slam down the tail of the board, sliding the side of your front foot along the board in a quick motion. I practice but my board just flips out from under me.

"Don't worry," says River. "You'll get it. It took me weeks and I only get an inch of air."

After we've been riding for about half an hour, River's pulls his vibrating phone from his pocket. "Make it so," he says into the phone. "Now? Can't I stay here? Oh, all right."

"I have to go," he says, and we go back inside.

"Want me to write the email letter to find your dad?" he asks after we clean up the computer area.

"Sure."

"You can translate it tomorrow, and then we'll send it. And I'll print it, too."

"Translate it?"

"Did you forget they speak Spanish in Mexico?" He laughs.

"Did you forget I don't speak Spanish?" Where does he get off assuming I'm bilingual?

"You don't?"

"No, I don't." I don't want to be Mexican. I don't want to be a Latina. I don't want to follow in my family's footsteps. Papi the traitor. Mami the deserted wife. Daniel the dropout. Danita the *quinceañera* queen.

"Why don't you work on it?" he tells me. "Preserve your culture. I'm learning Tagalog just so I might be able to talk to my Filipino relatives someday."

"Are you a genius or something?"

"No, it's my superpower. Everyone has a super-power."

"Superpower? Really? I think your first-grade friends are starting to rub off on you."

"It's true. People have unique abilities that can be almost like superhero powers."

"Not me." I'm embarrassed for River. It might be okay to believe you have a super power, if you keep it a secret. But people will really think you're weird if you talk about it.

"You might not know yours, yet. I didn't know mine at first. I thought I got ripped off. You know because of my . . ." He holds out his hands and then points to his ears. "But superheroes never know their power right away, right? Not Superman. Not Batman. Not Harry Potter."

I walk to the closet to get my coat. He's got me thinking about superpowers, even though it's super babyish. I'm pretty sure I'm the one who got ripped off. I'm fat and ugly with diabetes and I'm dumb, I mean stupid—no, I mean I need new strategies, like Yari said. Lots of them.

"If we don't get any information from our phone call to TAICO, we could take a trip to your dad's work next week and ask around," says River. "Find out if anybody knows what happened."

"Yah. We could find his friend José Villapando and ask him. They drove together everyday. He would know if they fired him for leaving to take care of my bisabuelita. And the lady who works in the office knows me. She might help."

River puts out his hand. And I don't even care. I shake it. I shake the two-finger hand of this weirdo-smart skateboarding detective who carves better than Danny's friend Freddie. River's two fingers squeeze the top of my hand and the shivers don't matter. Not at all. I separate my four fingers into a V. "Live long and prosper," I tell him. And he smiles the hugest smile, which makes my *pepita* of hope get a little flower bud.

"Hey," he says as I walk into the hall. "I forgot to tell you something."

"What?" I ask, noticing him rolling his hands together, his nervous thing, and I know what he's going to tell me.

"My tests came back and I'm starting at Robert Frost on Monday. Can you believe it? I'm finally done being a bus student."

"Awesome saucesome," I say, pretending to be excited. But a sign starts to flash inside my brain. NO. NO. OH NO. And some uh-ohs start to drip into the uh-oh bucket in my stomach.

"Fourth grade with a sign language interpreter and a speech therapist," he says, still nervously rolling.

"Maybe you'll be in my class," I say, still pretending, which is sort of close to lying.

"I hope so," he says.

"Me, too." I cross my fingers behind my back. I have so many feelings I can't even sort them all out. Happy for River. Worried for me. Ashamed for worrying. Embarrassed for being ashamed. And all these feelings after being so happy about my *pepita* of hope. Find an emoticon for all those feelings and I'll give you a million dollars.

CHAPTER NINE

D IS FOR DIFFERENT

Remember that spot-disappearing spray I'm inventing? I need it on Monday morning. Before I go to school. To spray all over me. So I can disappear. I hide out in the nurse's office, taking forever to put the alcohol on the cotton ball and find just the perfect place to poke myself. I don't want to see Noodlenose and I don't want to see River. I mean, I told him all kinds of personal stuff. About Papi and my diabetes. What if he blabs to everybody?

Okay, I'm just going to say it, even though it's "highly illogical," as River would say. I want to be friends with River at home, but not at school.

115

I'm just not the kind of person who sticks up for other people. Yet. Which is what you're supposed to say if you have Yari's growth mindset. I don't have any real friends at Robert Frost. Yet. And if I have to be River's helper friend I won't be able to make other friends. And the worst thing, if River acts weird with his Star Trek salute and his superpower stuff, I'll be super embarrassed for him and embarrassed we're friends. Yes, I do sound uncaring, unkind, and selfish. But I'm just not ready to be River's friend in public. Not yet.

When I see Mrs. Marsh I ask if she needs me to run any errands, but she says no thanks.

I act super interested in Mrs. Marsh's story so she'll keep talking. Her dog, Sniffer, loves to chase rabbits, but it turns out the black rabbit with a stripe down its back had a little surprise for poor Sniffer. And it's not the first time Sniffer's been sprayed by a skunk. He doesn't seem to remember the consequences when he spies something tempting.

"Maybe you should call him Smeller," I suggest.

"Good idea," says Mrs. Marsh. "And maybe we should all learn a lesson from Sniffer when we're tempted to do something we already know will hurt us."

I roll my eyes, because I know she's making a point. My black rabbit with a stripe down its back happened to be a jelly-filled doughnut I found in a box on the counter this morning. What? You know you would have wolfed it down just like me.

Mrs. Marsh points to my chart on her desk. "You know, DeeDee, you've been quite a regular lately. If you're struggling to stabilize, it might be a good idea to go back to the hospital. That happens sometimes in the beginning."

That's not going to happen to me, I think. No way. I don't know how Mami will pay for the medical bills without Papi's insurance. And how can River and I do our detective work if I'm in the hospital? "I'll be more careful," I say.

When I get back to the classroom, I hang up my coat and scan the labels above the coat hooks. Oh My Gatos. There it is. RIVER RAMOS-HENRY.

I slide into my seat as the bell rings, keeping my eyes on my homework folder. I sneak a quick look and see that River is sitting on the opposite side of the room, very near the front. Mrs. Cruella is talking to a bowling-pin-shaped lady with big hoop earrings over in the corner. The lady puts what looks like a flip phone on a black cord around Mrs. Cruella's neck.

Then they both talk to River while they push some buttons on the cell phone. River nods and the lady props herself up on the counter in the front of the room.

"Good morning everybody," says Mrs. Cruella. "We have a new student, River, in our class. Let's make him feel welcome." And while Mrs. Cruella talks, the lady waggles her hands all around. I'm not being mean, but she looks like a wobbling lunatic, and River isn't even looking at her.

"And because River is hard of hearing, we also have some resources that will help him be comfortable in our class. This is Miss Monaldo, a sign language interpreter, and this"—Mrs. Cruella points at the flip phone—"is an FM transmitter to bring my voice closer to River."

Nancy asks, "Why doesn't it sound any louder?"

Miss Monaldo moves her hands, signing Nancy's question for River. I don't get it. He understands just fine when I'm around him. Why does he need all these things?

Mrs. Cruella explains how the FM thing works and then she makes us all stand up and move our desks into a giant U shape. "This will be easier for River to be able to see who's talking so he can participate in the class."

When Mrs. Cruella isn't looking, I catch Samantha's eye and shake my hands like a maniac, making fun of Miss Monaldo. Samantha covers up a giggle with her hand. I feel River's eyes on me but I don't look at him. Except for our new seating arrangement and Miss Monaldo up in the front, our very own no-sound mime, things go about the same as usual.

During our class discussion of *Ragweed*, the new book we started, Noodlenose says she thinks the author should write about people and not mice. She talks extremely loud when she answers questions, until Mrs. Cruella tells her it's not necessary.

"Well, I want to make sure he can hear me," she says, pointing at River.

"I can hear you," River says. "And so can the kids in China."

Everybody laughs. Except Noodlenose. Good one, I think.

Then River says he read *Ragweed* last year, in third grade, and when authors give human traits to animals it's called anthropomorphism. "It makes us notice when Ragweed is a leader even though he's only a little mouse. Underdogs don't have to be bullied. If they stick together."

Good grief, I think.

At recess River kicks the soccer ball around with some kids. I climb up to the top of the jungle gym where nobody can bother me. It's hard not to notice River with his corkscrew spaghetti hair and his Bluetooth thingies, and when the ball flies past him onto the playground he runs right underneath me to get it. I see Nancy stick out her foot and trip him, but he doesn't fall.

"I had a good trip, thanks," he yells at her over his shoulder.

Colin runs up behind River and scrambles onto the first rung of the jungle gym. "Come on," he says.

River tosses him the ball but doesn't follow, just weaves around under the bars. Then it starts to drizzle and the lunch supervisors send us inside early.

At lunchtime, I quickly scoot between Hannah and Nicole, just in case River tries to sit near me. But he doesn't. He eats at the table with the other students who have teachers to help them. The kids with disabilities, who are different. And that's best, isn't it? I mean what if we have soup? The teachers at the special table can help him with his blue hand aid ball that holds any kind of tool, like a spoon or a pen. I can only see his back, and for just a second I wonder if anybody even asked him where he wanted to sit. Frosty school. Putting everybody in icy containers.

I never noticed all the kids at that table before. They're all different. Some are in wheelchairs. One has on a helmet. One girl sits and throws her head back and forth while the teacher tries to aim the food at her mouth.

I used to call those students handicapped, but River says they're not handicapped. They just have different capabilities, in the same way he does. Not disabilities. Not defects. Distinctions. It almost makes me want to go and sit with him. I shake the thought away. Not yet.

When it's time for peer tutoring, Yari squeals when she sees me. "OMG. That shirt looks amazing on you. Purple is so you."

We get down to business. After we finish going over all the vocabulary from the next chapter in *Ragweed*, she says, "Guess who I met this morning?" She starts to put everything into our tutoring folder. "The new kid in your class, River. Do you know him?"

I shake my head no, just slightly. What will Yari think of me if she knows I hang out with River? The needle on my truthometer wiggles and I squeeze my hands together.

"I took him on a tour of Robert Frost. He's so cool. And funny." Yari holds up her hand. "Live long and prosper," she says.

•

After school Mrs. Marsh needs to check my levels since they were off all day. And I have to wait, because she's talking to a parent. Finally, I trudge home in the drizzling, cold rain. Why are things so hard for me? Why am I different? I never even talked to River once at school. Not once. What kind of lousy neighbor am I? What is wrong with me? I open the door to our apartment. Danita, Andrea, and River are all inside, laughing hysterically. Yes, hysterically. And yes, River. In my apartment.

"Hi DeeDee," says Danita, gulping for air. "River's mom had an emergency at work, so he's going to wait here for his babysitter."

"Oh," I say. "What's so funny?"

"We were just talking about *quinceañeras*. River asked if we have one every year."

Everybody busts up laughing again. Everybody but me.

"*Ochoañera, nueveañera . . .*" snorts Andrea.

"*Diezañera, onceañera, doceañera . . .*" continues Danita.

"*Treceañera, catorceañera . . .*" says River.

"*Quinceañera,*" shout Danita and Andrea.

"I'll be right back," I say and head to the bathroom. Live long and prosper, you weirdos.

They're still talking about *quinceañeras* when I come back.

"So it's like a wedding," says River, "but nobody gets married? That's cool. Do we bring presents?"

I roll my eyes. "Really? Don't be so excited about it. I'm not."

"When is your Queen Sarah, Danita?" asks River.

Queen Bee doubles over laughing again. "Oh my gosh. That's great. You are too funny."

River's hard of hearing probably makes new Spanish words tricky. So he's probably not being funny. But of course Danita is clueless about what's hard for River.

Danita explains, "*Quinceañera. Quince* which means fifteen. And *añera* for the year. *Quince-añera.* It's in May."

Danita makes quesadillas for a snack. Rolling out the red carpet for River, like she never does for me. River and I do our homework. Or I should say, I do my homework because River finished almost all of his at school.

"It's so easy," he says.

I turn on the TV. Dancing with the Stars is on. "What do you want to watch?" I ask him.

"This," he says. "I love *Dancing with the Stars*."

Andrea says, "Danita, this song is so good. You should put it on your *quinceañera* playlist."

River stands up. "Come on, Danita, I know this one."

Guess who's left sitting on the couch while the three of them dance?

Finally Shondrea calls to let River know she's arrived, and he shoulders his backpack and heads out the door.

I follow him to the hallway. "Hey, want to skateboard later if the rain stops?"

The look he gives me is hard to figure out. A combination of confusion, doubt, and surprise. Definitely not on my emoticon face chart.

"Not today," he says. "And not tomorrow. I'm going to indoor soccer with Colin tomorrow."

"Oh, okay," I say. He made a friend on his first day? I've been at Frosty almost three weeks without an invitation.

"Maybe Thursday. If my mom's appointment with Mrs. Krewell doesn't take too long."

"Okay, only if you can squeeze me in," I say.

He gives me the same weird face and slams the door without his Vulcan salute.

What's his deal? Just because I didn't talk to him today? I really didn't have much of a chance. A leaf on my *pepita* plant of hope falls off and I go back inside my apartment.

"Hey DeeDee," says Danita. "If you really don't want to come to my *quinceañera*, I can invite River instead."

"He'd love it," says Andrea.

I go to the kitchen and pour myself a glass of milk. I squirt in chocolate syrup until my fingers get tired. I stir. The spoon hits the side of the glass. Clink. Clink. Clink. Fourth grade stinks. Clink. Clink. Clink. My sister stinks. Clink. Clink. Clink. My whole life stinks. I grab my helmet and pads and take my skateboard outside. I push and cruise, practicing my turning and getting faster. I'm really shredding when I see Mrs. Robinson at the end of the sidewalk waving at me. I zip back around and drag my foot to slow down.

"Do you know how to read?" she asks me in a huffy voice.

"Yes, but—" I start.

"No skateboarding," she says and huffs off before I can explain. Well la-di-da. I guess River's the only one with skateboarding privileges. I guess it's different for me.

•

On Tuesday and Wednesday I watch River work his magic at Robert Frost. Mrs. Krewell frowns at the hullabaloo his group makes during their group project on *Ragweed*, but when she walks over to see what's happening, she laughs. Sour-puss actually laughs.

"It was River's idea," says Colin.

Every day Miss Monaldo follows River around to art, gym, music, and signs for him even when he's not watching. Seems kind of like a waste of time and money to me.

At recess, River and Colin organize the soccer lovers into teams and have a little mini-game that Colin calls a scrimmage. All they ever used to do was kick the ball wildly across the field and chase after it until the lunch bell rang. Before River. From my perch up on the jungle gym I think about it. River's already a planet in the solar system, while I'm just a black hole.

Both days at lunch I notice River talking to Yari. Smiling and laughing. Ridiculous.

Mrs. Cruella moved my tutoring to before school because Yari has fifth-grade testing. Yari told me her best friend invited her to a water park for a birthday party and all her friends are going. Right. All her friends. Which means, well, I don't have to tell you what it means.

Noodlenose Nancy and Despicable Me Sherie find ways to be sneaky-mean to River. When Mrs. Cruella says "Give me five," Noodlenose whispers, "Or three if you're River," and Sherie giggles. Whenever River leaves the room to go to speech therapy, they make the Vulcan salute at his back and a couple of the boys copy them, snickering. Noodlenose still talks super loud to River, even though Mrs. Cruella told her not to.

Thursday, without warning, it snows, and my gym shoes turn into ice blocks by the time I get home. And it's still chilly in our apartment even though Danny called the manager to complain. Danita huddles in her fleece jacket, madly texting someone on her phone.

"Why don't you go play with River?" asks Danita.

"Where's Andrea?" I ask.

"Decorating valentine cookies. For the fundraiser."

Poor Danita. Stuck here with me. She never goes anywhere anymore.

"How's *quinceañeara* planning?"

"I dunno if I'm even going to have one." She turtles her neck into her jacket.

Oh My Gatos. If I don't find Papi soon, our family won't have any pepitas of hope left.

I turn on Dancing with the Stars and start my math homework. Danita sniffles and goes off to her bedroom. I jump when a blam-blam-blam smacks against the door.

"Come on," River shouts at me when I open the door. In a Yoda voice he says, "Paper we got, valentines we make!"

"Going to River's," I yell and grab the key. Just saying that makes a sunny spot in my heart. I hope this means River's decided he's okay with being friends in private.

Sheets of assorted pink and red paper fan out across his coffee table—Pink, Scarlet, and Wild Strawberry. River's markers sit in the middle of the paper, with two bags of Tootsie Pops.

"Holy jalapeño," I say.

"My mom printed the list of names Mrs. Krewell sent out," he says. "If you want to personalize."

"What list?"

"She attached it to the weekly newsletter she emails to our parents."

"Oh," I say. I'm almost positive Mrs. Cruella never asked me or Mami for our email addresses. Danny checks our email when he's at school because we don't have a computer in our house. Yet. Does Mrs. Cruella think we're so different we can't get email?

For two hours we cut and paste hearts into bigger hearts and attach lollipops.

"How was soccer?" I ask. I saw a poster Mrs. Marsh put up for Valentine's Day. Two teddy bears hugging. Across the top of the poster it says, THE ONLY WAY TO HAVE A FRIEND IS TO BE ONE. RALPH WALDO EMERSON. And if two teddy bears can learn to be friends, then for sure people can, can't they? I mean, does a bear poop in the woods?

"Great," River says. "And different. I'm not used to being around all hearing people."

"Must be weird," I say.

"Yah. And Robert Frost is different than I thought," he says, holding up a multi-layered heart valentine. In the middle River drew a fancy arrow sticking into the tiniest, red-checked, center heart. YOU HIT THE BULL'S-EYE, he wrote.

"Different how?" I ask.

"The equipment, for one thing. It's not adaptive, so people with disabilities have few choices for recess. For example, the jungle gym. If it had rubber hand holds or triangular sections, I'd be able to climb it. Also, the teachers seem confused about diversity. Like Mr. Bronton, our gym teacher."

"You mean Mr. Incredible?" I ask and River snorts. "He thinks diabetics can't exercise."

"Do you have a different name for everybody?" he asks.

"No, not everybody. Just the people who deserve them," I say.

River goes on, "And there's not a lot of diversity. No Filipinos. No Middle Eastern kids. And not many multi-racial kids. It doesn't seem as accepting as my old school."

"Noodlenose Nancy is Chinese," I say.

"Noodlenose? She probably deserves that nick-name. How do you know she's Chinese?" River asks.

"Uh, I just thought she was."

"She could be Asian-American, or Japanese, Chinese, Korean, Vietnamese—"

"Okay, I'm not sure." I hate it when he acts all know-it-all. Then I say, "But maybe it takes time for some people to get used to differences. I used to think Mrs. Cruella hated Mexicans but Yari says Mrs. Cruella has high expectations for everybody."

"It's weird when you expect people to act one way and they act another, isn't it?" River gives me that strange look again.

I change the subject. "What's the next thing we should do to find my Papi?"

He pulls one of the computers from the shelf under the coffee table. "I wrote the email. I'll print it for you to translate. And if you still want to go to his work . . ."

"Of course I want to. Does a bear—"

"—poop in the woods?" River finishes my sentence. "I can't tomorrow. I have a date."

"A date?" Flames shoot into my head. I need my own ice castle where I can hide from everyone.

"With my mom. I've taken her out for Valentine's Day since I was three."

My blood pressure goes back to normal. "Oh, well, that's nice. But Valentine's Day is on Saturday."

"She has a real date on Saturday," River says and raises his eyebrows. "And Monday Danny said I could ride along to the high school when he picks up his test results. The parking lot is great for skateboarding."

I see red flames again. Danny? And River? Skateboarding at Northlake High School? "My brother Danny?" I choke out.

"You can come if you want," River says.

"Okay," I say, glad I didn't open my mouth and let the flames out.

"And I tried calling TAICO, but they don't give out information on the phone."

That little sunny spot in my heart gets warm, knowing River tried.

He goes on. "So we can try Tuesday, or maybe Friday, to go to your dad's work."

"I think it's kind of far away. I used to go there with my dad sometimes."

"Yah. We have to take the bus. I already checked." River shows me a map on his laptop. "I'll print this later." He leans close and whispers, "And FYI I'm not going to tell my mom. She'll ask too many questions."

"Oh, me either," I say, glad he always thinks ahead.

"I don't lie, so we'll say we're going to the library and we'll just go to TAICO first."

"Deal," I say and pack up my valentines. "Thanks for doing valentines with me."

"The honor is mine," he says in the Matrix voice he and Mr. Hawaii used at the hospital.

CHAPTER TEN

D IS FOR DINOSAUR

On Friday morning Mrs. Cruella lets us pass out our valentines first thing in the morning.

When we're done passing them out, Mrs. Cruella tells us we can read our cards during reading time, since most of them will have figurative language or poetry. But lots of them have candy and you can't read that, so I eat it instead. Who doesn't eat valentine candy? I don't even think about it when I pop the two little packets of red and pink jelly beans into my mouth.

And not too long after that, Mrs. Cruella sends me to Mrs. Marsh because I'm dizzy and sleepy. Not too many kids notice, but River's eyebrows bunch together like he's worried. And when Mrs. Cruella asks who wants to accompany DeeDee to the nurse, Nancy mumbles, "Not again."

Mrs. Marsh goes ballistic when she tests me. Do you know how many carbs they pack into one little, teensy jelly bean? Mrs. Marsh says about one gram. And one packet has twenty-five jelly beans. So, since I ate two whole packets of jelly beans, I ate fifty grams of carbs.

"Dinora Diaz, you know better than to eat that much sugar. You can't cheat. You can't pretend you can do what everyone else can do. Your diabetes will always tattle on you," scolds Mrs. Marsh.

I hate not being able to do what I want. I hate not being like everybody else. And I hate diabetes. By The Way.

Mrs. Marsh keeps scolding. "I've told you so many times. Balance your diet and stay active. If you don't, you'll end up in the hospital."

"I'm very active. In fact, I'm going to sign up for the Spring Fling thing," I tell Mrs Marsh. Who does she think she is?

"Oh, DeeDee. That's a wonderful idea. What are you going to do?"

"I'm choosing between skateboarding and dancing."

"You should definitely try out," she says. Her mood has totally flipped. "The Student Leadership Team only chooses one student from each grade level in each category. And you know"—Mrs. Marsh leans close to me—"Nancy Wang always dances. You should skateboard. You'll be such a good example of how to rise above your disability and inspire others."

Here's what I want to say: I just want to do it because I like to skateboard and dance. Isn't that enough? Why do I have to be somebody's motivation? I think about River. He would hate hearing that. I hate hearing it, too. But I don't say anything to Mrs. Marsh. She's not the kind of person who says things to be mean.

Instead I say, "Seriously. Diabetes can just get in line."

Mrs. Marsh laughs. "I'll stop by the office later and put your name on the tryout list."

"Okay," I say. Oh My Gatos. Why did I open my mouth? No matter what I decide to do, I won't be good enough to make it. Well, I don't have to go to the tryouts if I don't want to, do I?

I give Mrs. Cruella the note Mrs. Marsh wrote telling her to be more careful, but Mrs. Cruella tells me it's my responsibility and not hers. I guess somebody should tell that to my poor lollipop and the conversation hearts left in my valentine bag.

When we saw Dr. Zebra-Face last week, she told me I was adjusting as expected and will grow up to be a healthy young lady who has no limits to her activities.

So there, Mr. Incredible and Noodlenose Nancy. So there, Mrs. Marsh. But I miss Mami bringing pizza for late night binges, and Doritos and M&M's for snacks.

When I finally settle back into my desk, I see one of my valentines sticking out of my bag. I glance around.

Noodlenose Nancy sneers at me. "Somebody has a crush on you. The two misfits. What a pair."

Talk about flames shooting in my head and out of my mouth. I'm out of my seat and heading toward Nancy when Mrs. Cruella says, "Give me five."

"JW," I mouth at Nancy. Just wait.

"What?" she mouths back. But I don't answer.

•

At recess on Monday I try to talk to Nicole and Samantha. Try to have a friend by being one. "Thanks for the valentines," I say.

"I'm sorry I put candy in yours. I forgot," says Samantha.

"That's okay. I'm not sure a cheeseburger and fries would have fit."

They both laugh. We're sitting on the second level of the jungle gym.

Noodlenose yells up to me, "Hey, what kind of dinosaur are you, Dinora? A T-Rex or a Brontosaurus?"

I don't get it at first, and then I freeze. Nancy found out my name. My real name, Dinora Diaz. Someone told her. And who's the only person who could have done that? River.

"Why don't you answer me, Dinora Dinosaura?" she yells, and then she runs away with Sherie following her.

Nicole giggles. "That's funny. Is that your name?"

"No. It's Dee-nor-a." Only my lips move because my teeth are clenched so tight I can barely spit it out.

I scramble down from the bars and look around for River. He's kicking the soccer ball around. I wait on the edge of the field for the bell to ring, my hate making me very hot and sweaty. When he walks toward me I glare at him, sending nasty messages with my eyes.

"What?" he says when he gets close enough, smiling at me with a smudge of mud on his cheek and his knee.

"How could you?"

"What?" he says again, but without a smile this time.

"You told Nancy my name."

River throws out his arms. "I didn't. I swear. I would never do that. I keep my promises." One dark eyebrow goes low over his eye and his forehead crinkles into four up and down lines, as if pressed with a fork.

"Then how did she know?"

"I don't know. It wasn't me." River shakes his spa-ghetti-noodle hair. "I haven't said anything to your friends. Even though they pick on me all the time."

"Nancy and Sherie aren't my friends."

"Oh yah? Then why do you sit with them? Why do you want to be friends at home and ignore me at school?" He starts to walk away, then turns back. "You're a two-faced liar!"

I have that squeezy pinch in my stomach and it stays there all through lunch, where I sit at the end of the table, almost falling off the bench onto the floor, watching River out of the corner of my eye as he has fun with the kids and teachers at his table. "Two-faced liar," echoes in my ears over and over. I see Yari sit down next to him and they lean their heads together and point excitedly at Yari's notebook. And the whole time I'm watching them, I'm wondering how in the jalapeño Nancy knows my real name.

Noodlenose thinks she's hysterical when she bumps her tray into me on the way to the garbage, and says, "Oh excuse me, Dinora."

The other kids near me ask, "Is that your name? Dinora?"

I try to keep calm. I wish I was River. He'd know what to do. He'd make it a joke. He'd be cool. But when Nancy says, "Are you sure you should try out for Spring

Fling? I didn't know dinosaurs could dance," I can't take it. I push her. Hard. And she falls.

I lean my face down and scream so loud drops of spit fly out of my mouth. "Leave me alone." I tear out of the room without waiting for her to get up or yell back.

I run into Mrs. Marsh when I turn the corner and I almost knock her down. "Whoa. What's the matter, Dinora?" She steers me toward her office, past the SPRING FLING sign-up sheet. And there, on the sign-up sheet, in Mrs. Marsh's handwriting, I see DINORA DIAZ—UNDECIDED. The first name on the list. And down a few names I see NANCY WANG, DANCE, in Nancy's loopy writing.

Smack, it hits me. River didn't tell Nancy my real name. Mrs. Marsh signed Dinora and not DeeDee up for tryouts.

I don't say anything to Mrs. Marsh. It's not her fault. It's my fault. For having such a horrible name. For being such a horrible friend. And for blaming River, who's never been horrible to anybody. I sulk off to class after listing off everything I ate to Mrs. Marsh.

"Don't forget, tryouts are in about three weeks," she calls after me.

Not for me, I think. Not on your life.

•

I feel ugly the rest of the afternoon, frizzy-frayed from the windy recess, sticky-sweaty from running down the hall, and itchy-scritchy from my too-tight sweatshirt. Mrs. Cruella calls me over and tells me I made positive growth on the last reading test but I'm still in the red zone. She's moving me up to a reading group in Mr. Somerset's room, so I will switch classes, just for reading.

Under my breath I say, "Once a dunce, always a dunce." And when us dunces switch rooms, I notice River getting moved up to be with the advanced literacy group.

I remember a joke Danny told me. "When God was handing out smarts, you thought he said farts, and said no thank you, I'm already full of them." It makes me feel better, thinking about Danny. He never gives up. Working and going to night school, plus all his training in NGYCP. If his GED scores are good enough, he can apply for a special training program. Papi would be so proud. I wonder if River's too mad to go with me and Danny to high school tonight.

And thinking about Danny and Papi makes me straighten up a bit. I'm doing better. I am. I might catch up to River and be in the advanced reading group next year. Right?

"Where's River?" asks Danny when I walk through the door.

"I don't know," I say.

We wait for a bit. Danny texts him. We wait some more.

"I don't think River can go," I say finally. He's mad for sure, and I don't blame him. I am Dinora Dinosaura and I should be extinct.

"Are you sure?" Danny says.

"Yah. It's okay," I say, "we can go without him." If River's mad at me, I don't need Danny taking his side.

Danny gives me a odd look and picks up his keys from the table. "Okay. But remember what Papi says. *"Amistades verdaderas, mantienen las puertas abiertas,"* Always keep your door open for a true friend.

"It's not that," I say. "Nothing's wrong. I think he probably forgot." Danny sure has a lot of memories of Papi. I hope Papi comes home soon. I want more memories.

We're in front of River's door when it opens and he pops out. "Hey," he says. "I was just coming over. Phone problems."

"Oh, well, we were just coming to get you," I say.

"We sure were," says Danny, staring at me like I've lost my marbles.

River sits up front with Danny and they talk about their scores from NBA 2K18, the last video game they played. Nobody talks to me. When we get to Northlake, Danny shows River the soccer fields where he used to play. Then he goes inside and leaves us in the empty parking lot with our skateboards.

"Were you guys leaving without me?" River asks once Danny's gone.

"I thought you didn't want to go," I say, my stomach giving me little pinchy squeeze again.

"Why?" asks River.

"Because you're mad at me."

"I am mad at you, but that doesn't mean I don't want to hang out with you. We're friends. We're still going to your dad's work next week, aren't we?" He does a running start to get on his skateboard and I push-shove after him. We both ride with our left foot front. Most of the snow and slush has been plowed from the parking lot, and it's smooth with no speed bumps.

I make it around the parking lot, only bailing once, keeping loose and rolling out, like River taught me. And yes, I'm wearing my helmet and so is River. Total geek look, but Dr. Zebra-Face scared the jalapeño right out of me when she saw skateboarding bruises at my checkup. "You have a long life ahead of you," she said. "Let's do what we can to keep everything attached to your body."

River practices his kick turn, and the new tic-tacs, which are little mini kick turns that make you go really fast. No matter how hard I try to do them I always lean too far and the back of my board hits the ground—wipe out.

Neither of us can skate switch and fakie. River says all the good skaters need to be comfortable skating switch and fakie on ramps. He also says someday, when it gets warmer and I get a little more confident, his mom will take us to the huge skatepark that's halfway between my new apartment and my old trailer park.

A few cars pull into the parking lot, dropping off kids in tights carrying slippers. I skate closer and River follows me.

"Prestige Academy of Dance," River says. "I used to take lessons there."

Danny comes out of the door as two little pink-tutu girls skip through. He points to his car and we skate around the growing line of cars to meet him.

"What kind of classes do you take here, Danny? Ballet?" I ask.

"Very funny, Gordita," he says and pokes me. "Guess what? GED with honors."

River and I high-five him. "That's so sick," I say.

River laughs. "You sound like Yari." We jump into Danny's car. "I forgot to tell you. Yari invited me to be on SLT, to represent kids with disabilities." He says it as if it's no big deal, but I can tell it's a big deal to him.

"You're not going to do it, are you? Only fifth graders are on SLT. Didn't you say you hate being inspiring?"

"Of course I'm going to do it. It's not being an inspiration, it's representation. Someone has to make sure our rights aren't violated and we have equal access."

I'm confused. I thought River didn't want to identify with disabled people. That's why he transferred to Robert Frost. I thought he only had distinctions, not disabilities. Now, all of a sudden he wants to be the poster child? I think about what Mrs. Marsh said to me about being an inspiration and how I felt cheated. I guess I don't understand the difference between inspiration and representation.

River pulls up his jacket sleeve. "All the SLT members wear these," he says. "The colors represent the school's mission."

And there on his wrist is the same string bracelet Yari wears every day. I pretend to be fascinated by the line of cars through my suddenly blurry eyes. And for some reason when I see the soccer field as we leave the parking lot it makes me even blurrier, remembering Danny scoring the winning goal in his last ever game. Everything was normal then. I like normal.

River just keeps talking to Danny. "So the mission is 'to create an inclusive community of lifelong learners.' That's what the knot stands for. Then each color represents one way to do that. Yellow for critical thinking. Orange for imagination and joy. Green for growth. Blue for honesty and loyalty. And red for global citizenship."

"Way cool," says Danny. "That reminds me of some things from my National Guard training."

"Maybe I'll join the National Guard someday," says River.

And maybe I'll throw up all over the inside of Danny's car.

CHAPTER ELEVEN

D IS FOR DENIAL

Yari's bracelet is just about the ugliest bracelet I've ever seen. I almost tell her so during tutoring on Tuesday morning.

She puts her finger on a word I've missed ten times. "It's a French word, DeeDee. French words have to be pronounced differently." She writes BOUQUET. "This is boo-kay. Not bow-ket." She writes BOUTIQUE. "And this is boo-teek. As in Sun and Stars Boutique, where I like to shop. Not bow-ti-kway."

I try the new word again. "Desper-ray." I tap my foot. I can't concentrate.

"Almost. Des-per-row. I'm going to print you a list of all the French words so you can sound really smart, okay?" Yari hits a few buttons on the computer and zips to the printer to get the printout.

I reach down and unclip one of the pom-poms from her backpack. The purple one. It's a thing with the fifth-grade girls. Clip-on pom-poms. Much better than an ugly string bracelet.

•

"Free to the first taker!" shouts Noodlenose Nancy at the lunch table, and she holds her bag of popcorn up in the air.

I grab the bag. I love popcorn.

"I didn't mean you." Noodlenose snatches it back from me. "I'm sure popcorn isn't on your diabetes diet," she says in a snotty voice.

I pull it back. "Why don't you get a nose job?" I scream at her.

"Oh look, everybody. PeePee's getting mad." Noodlenose whacks the popcorn, but I hang on tight and my arm knocks over Sherie's chocolate milk.

"Stop it," yells Sherie and jumps up from the table.

"Sorry," I tell Sherie.

"No wonder you only have freaks for friends!" Nancy tugs at the popcorn.

"You're a freak!" I tug back.

"Not like your friend River!"

Before I think I blurt out, "He's not my friend."

"Oh yah? Then what were you doing in the high school parking lot with him?"

Bull-Face rushes over. "What's going on?"

"DeeDee stole my popcorn." Pretend tears squeeze from Noodlenose Nancy's eyes.

"She spilled my milk." Sherie points at her jeans and the chocolate milk pouring onto the floor.

"That's not what happened, you liar." I throw the bag at Noodlenose, and popcorn rains down on the table.

"I want this cleaned up," says Bull-Face, spitting out each consonant and folding her arms across her chest.

"No." I sit down. "It wasn't my fault."

"DeeDee, you clean this up, now," says Bull-Face with a louder voice, coming close to my side of the table.

Noodlenose picks at the popcorn. Despicable Me Sherie sops up milk with a napkin. I sit.

"Did you hear me? Clean. This. Up." Bull-Face puts her hands on the table and gets down at my eye level. And for the first time in history the lunchroom is deadly quiet. The kids with their backs to the action swivel their heads like owls and the far-away ones half stand up, craning their necks like geese. One pair of eyes leaps out at me, intense and pleading. Yari. She's shaking her head slightly. She wants me to stop making trouble. But I can't. I'm over the edge. I can't back up.

"No. It. Wasn't. My. Fault," I stand up and scream back at Bull-Face.

Her face is plum purple. And with her lips pulled back from her teeth, the way a dog with rabies might look, she snarls at me, "Go to the office. Now."

I march away. Past the other fourth-grade table. Past the first-grade table. Past the special-needs table. Past the fifth-grade table. Yari stares at me. The tops of my ears are hot. I'm going to explode in one minute.

I turn right and run down a hall. I slip into the first bathroom I pass and lock the stall door. I pull my legs up on the seat and I break my no-crying rule. Why didn't I just ignore Noodlenose? Why did I grab the popcorn anyway? Why didn't I pay attention to Yari? Why did I say River wasn't my friend? What is my problem?

I don't believe in best friends. Not anymore. I don't even believe in friends.

Friends tell each other secrets. I told River about my dad. And I'm the only one that knows River's thumb used to be his big toe. The only one ever. Besides his mom and the medical people, of course. And I promised I would always keep his secret. But then I go and lie about being his friend. He doesn't even need me for a friend. He's got so many friends. Even my family is stealing him away from me.

Friends stick up for each other. When he comes to my house we whisper about Queen Bee and Andrea behind their backs. He eats healthy snacks that are okay for me to eat. And he doesn't care if I'm not skinny. He hates being skinny. He even learned how to say a few things in Spanish for Mami and she loves him. But then I go and pretend I'm not even his friend.

When I die, my tombstone will say, Dinora Diaz, worst friend in the world, the girl who didn't deserve a best friend.

After I've been in the bathroom awhile, my back hurts from the toilet pipes. Kids start to come in to use the bathroom. I stay quiet and watch their feet. I begin to notice some pretty big feet. This must be the fifth-grade bathroom. And then I realize I see only Jordans and Nikes and Vans. Something starts to nag at me. Where are the fluffy boots? Where are the sparkly, light-up shoes? And the pink high-tops? I peek through the crack in the door and a bucket of uh-oh spreads over my insides. Oh My Gatos. I'm in the boy's bathroom.

I wish for Harry Potter's invisibility cloak. I wish for Superman's cape. I wish for Ant-Man's super-suit. My legs go to sleep and get the prickles. I lean my head against the stall wall. I'm dizzy and I think I have that phobia of tiny spaces, claus-something. How can I just walk out of the boy's bathroom?

Sitting on a toilet sure makes you thirsty. And hungry. I realize I didn't even finish my lunch. It seems as if

I've been in here for hours. Has it been hours? If only this day would end.

I hear a rustling from my pocket when I shift on my seat. I pull out a folded up paper. The Google map River printed with the bus directions to TAICO. I almost gasp out loud. Oh My Gatos! I forgot until right this minute that today was the day we were going to take the bus to my papi's workplace. If I get in trouble for fighting I'll get grounded and time is slipping away for finding Papi before Danita's *quinceañera*.

I make a decision. I'm going to run home. Danny can call the school and say I'm sick. When Danny goes to work I'll wait for River at the bus stop. If he doesn't come, I'll go by myself. Papi will be so grateful when I find him. "Oh DeeDee, what a beautiful, smart young lady you've turned into," he'll say. He'll forget that I'm a disappointing, disagreeable daughter.

I wait until I see no feet at the sinks or the hole in the wall where the boys pee. Then I unlock the bathroom door. I'm half out the door when a boy runs smack into me. We both scream and I rush past him.

I need my backpack. My key is in my backpack. Does this hall connect to the fourth-grade hall? Nothing seems familiar but the exit signs. EXIT. EXIT. EXIT. I turn around and start to run toward the lunchroom. If I go back that way, I will know where I am. But I'm so woozy I have to slow down. I close my eyes and lean

against the wall. Red letters blink in my head. EXIT.
E. X. I. T. E . . X . . I . . T . . . E . . . X . . . I . . . T . . .

"DeeDee?" pants Mrs. Marsh in front of my face.
"Oh, my. They've been looking for you everywhere."
She grabs my arm. "DeeDee? Can you hear me? Did
you eat your lunch?"

I shake my head.

"Come on. Lean on me. Let's get you checked."

I don't remember walking to her office, but now
I'm lying on the paper-coated couch-bed. Mrs. Marsh
quickly pricks and scans and tut-tuts at the reading.
"Oh, dear. You're low. Very low. Here, drink this." She
calls the secretaries and tells them I'm in her office.
"Give her about ten minutes," she says into the phone.
"Then I'll walk her over."

When I walk into the principal's office, Mami and
Mrs. Cruella are holding hands. Both have red eyes and
tissues in their hands. I feel more of the uh-oh bucket
spreading into my heart. Noodlenose Nancy and
Despicable Me Sherie are sitting in chairs looking very
serious and scared. Behind them I see another lady that
must be somebody's mom.

The principal stands up. Mami rushes over to me
and gets all mushy in Spanish. "*Mija. Mija, pobrecita.
Estaba preocupado por ti.* I'm worried about you. *Me asus-
taste.* You scared me." She pats my cheek and strokes
my hair from my forehead.

The principal puts her arm around Mami. "I'm so sorry," she says.

I try to remember if I've ever met this principal. I look at the name plate on the desk. Dr. Hien Souriyavongsa. Huh. Nope. Doesn't ring a bell. Principal Sorry is about all I can figure out in the fog I'm in.

"DeeDee," she says to me. "We've all been very worried. We thought you ran away from school. Where were you?"

"The bathroom." My voice sounds very small and soft. Mousy. Not at all my voice.

"We looked in all the bathrooms. We've had a search going on. We called the police."

The uh-oh bucket is really overflowing now. "I was in the fifth-grade bathroom. The boys' bathroom." I see Noodlenose's eyes get wide. "By mistake."

"Well." Principal Sorry's mouth almost smiles. "Next time we'll have to do a better job of looking absolutely everywhere. Now, I've heard everyone's side of the story but yours. Maybe you could tell me later. Right now, Mrs. Marsh says you're a little under the weather. At this school we don't tolerate bullying or bully bystanders." She raises her eyebrows at Nancy and Sherie. "Can you explain what those words mean, girls?"

They both bob their heads up and down.

Nancy answers first. "A bully hurts people with words or actions over and over."

Then Sherie says, "And a bully bystander watches and doesn't help."

"Now, girls," says Principal Sorry. "Do you have something to take care of?"

Noodlenose Nancy stands up. "I'm sorry, DeeDee."

Sherie stands up next to her. "I'm sorry, too."

The lady behind them turns to Mami. "It seems our girls have gotten off on the wrong foot. Nancy is having some friends for a sleepover a week from Friday and she'd love to invite DeeDee. Wouldn't you, Nancy?"

My stomach stops its uh-oh spillover for a second. Sleepover? Did I hear that right? But Nancy's mom is inviting me, not Nancy. Beggars can't be choosers. That's what Danita says.

Nancy bounces her head up and down, like a puppet. "Yes, I would," she says in an I-will-do-whatever-you-say-so-I-can-live-another-day voice.

Mami claps her hands as though she's won the lottery.

Holy jalapeño, I think.

"Wonderful," says Principal Sorry. "I believe this coming Friday you three will have lunch detention together. It will be a good time to plan the sleepover."

Mami and I ride the bus home because I'm too dizzy to walk. Mami is not happy with me. "Too much trouble, *mija*. Too much," she tells me. "No make trouble." She reaches in her purse and pulls out a phone.

Not a new phone. But still, a phone. "Use for emergency. Danny fixed all up."

"What's my number?" I ask Mami, and she shows me.

"Call me," I say.

"For emergency."

"Just once, please."

My new-to-me phone rings. Danny set the theme song from *American Idol* for my ringtone. I press the red circle to stop the ringing. I know Mami is thinking the same thing I am. The *American Idol* song makes us miss Papi.

"Where's Papi?" I whisper, staring at the phone.

She pats my knee and shakes her head but doesn't answer me.

My head hurts from the noisy pling-plang bell as the bus announces each stop every two blocks. I try to fall asleep. After the fourth stop the speaker announces, "Next stop. Fairview Avenue," and we get off.

I think about asking about Papi again. Maybe Mami didn't want to talk about it in public. Maybe it's too shocking. Or maybe she really doesn't know. But then my mind wanders and I start worrying about the sleepover. We both plop down on the couch, exhausted. Mami closes her eyes and I snuggle next to her. Two seconds and she's sleep-breathing, both our bodies rising and falling.

I remember when Mami didn't work two jobs. I remember when she sat in the community room at the trailer park and talked with her friends. And went to Parent Academy English classes at Lincoln with the other moms. Everything's changed for her, too.

A few minutes later, Danita and Andrea come tromping in with River right behind them.

"What happened to you?" he asks. "You never came back from lunch." Then he puts his finger to his lips when he sees Mami sleeping next to me.

"I don't feel so good."

"Oh." He sounds disappointed "Maybe we can go to the library on Friday. I can't go Thursday." Library is our code word for bus trip.

Mami shifts next to me and opens her eyes. "DeeDee go over to sleep at her friend's house Friday," she tells River. Then she gets up to get ready for work.

"Not this Friday. Next Friday," I tell River.

"Ooh. Your first sleepover, DeeDee!" yells Danita as she and Andrea head toward the bedroom.

"*Callate*," I yell after her, forgetting again that I'm not speaking Spanish.

"Something crazy happened at school," says River. "The police showed up. Mrs. Cruella went to the office."

"It was me. I got in a fight at lunch. The whole lunchroom heard."

"Really? Well, not me. I can't hear anything in that lunchroom." River sits down on the couch. "Fight with who?"

So I tell him about Noodlenose Nancy and Despicable Me Sherie and how I refused to let her or the lunch supervisor, Bull-Face, push me around. "Bull-Face totally screamed in my face, and not in their faces. It's 'cause she hates Mexicans."

"She hates Mexicans just like Mrs. Cruella?" River squints his eyes at me.

"I said Mrs. Cruella didn't understand Mexicans. That's different."

It really bugs me when River acts all high and mighty. Bull-face is prejudiced, not me.

River stares at me, eyebrows raised.

"Do you want to hear what happened or not?"

River pretends to lock his lips and nods.

I tell him about the lunch detention and how I got invited to a sleepover at Noodlenose Nancy's house. I have a little hiccup in my throat as I leave out the part about telling my lunch table I'm not his friend and refusing to follow Bull-face's directions.

"You're going to Nancy's house? Yari's been doing all this research because of the new SLT inclusive community mission, and she found a newspaper article about Northlake High School graduation. Nancy's brother was the first Asian kid to attend Robert Frost. I'm the first Filipino."

"Nancy's got a brother?" I ask. I never knew that. But then, I never talk to Nancy because she's a noodlenose.

"Yari's making a PowerPoint about all the great things people say about Robert Frost. Nancy's brother was the valedictorian. That's the student with the highest grades."

"I know what a valedictorian is," I say. Boy I hate it when he gets all high-and-mighty.

"He thanked his teachers at Robert Frost for helping him achieve his dream. He got the Gates Scholarship. You know, Bill Gates? The inventor of Microsoft? I mean that's huge. He must be a genius. And he set records in track and was the student body vice president."

"Well, maybe Nancy's not related to her brother," I say, thinking that I wouldn't vote for Nancy if she was running for bear-poop scooper.

River busts out laughing. "I see what you mean," he says.

Mami bustles by us on her way out the door to work. "*Calladitos*," she says and points to Danita's bedroom, as if they actually might be studying.

River whispers, "*Calladitos*."

I show him my new-to-me phone. He shows me how to add contacts, starting with River Ramos-Henry, complete with a selfie he adds to the screen for his contact info.

"You can always put your friends in and add their phone numbers later. Look, here's how you edit." He touches a few spots and adds my phone number to the contact for River Ramos-Henry. Then he pulls out his expensive-looking phone and calls me. When my phone rings, his picture shows up with my phone number.

"Hi," I say into my new-to-me phone. "You've reached River the Geek. I'm programming phones right now so leave it at the beep."

He laughs and grabs my phone, deleting my number from his contact.

"I've had a phone ever since I can remember," he says.

"Lucky." Mami only has a flip phone. Danny and Danita have okay phones, but not iPhones, which they want.

River shows me the settings on his phone. "It's sort of a life-saving device for me. I even keep it under my pillow at night in case there's a fire."

"But won't you hear the smoke alarm?" I'm glad we heard the smoke alarm when my trailer burned down.

"I might not hear anything." River taps his ears. "So it's set on ring and vibrate. Call me."

I press River's contact picture and his phone rings and buzzes. His voicemail message comes on, "Make it so. Live long and prosper."

We start working on a half-finished puzzle of crayons, all lined up in rainbow rows. It's the hardest puzzle ever. River pushes the pieces around with his fused fingers, then slides the piece he wants to the edge so he can grab it. He's never wrong when he thinks a piece will fit into a spot. He's so smart, it's spooky.

"What's the word for having guts in Spanish?" he asks me.

"I don't know. I don't speak Spanish."

"Stop saying that. Now you can look up how to spell the Spanish words you need to translate the letter I wrote."

"Okay. I will." I almost forgot about the letters we're sending to Mexico.

"Now, what's guts in Spanish."

"Maybe *bella?*"

River speaks to his phone. "Meaning of *bella.*"

His phone speaks back. "Beautiful."

He kicks me. "Not funny."

"Hey, Danita," he yells. "How do you say brave in Spanish? Like gutsy?"

"*Diabla,*" Danita shouts back.

"Doesn't that mean devil?" asks River.

"Exactly!" Danita pokes her head out and points at me.

Andrea walks into the hall and reads from her phone. "*Activo. Desafiadora. Dinámico.*"

"Do you speak Spanish?" asks River.

"No, but I speak Google," says Andrea.

"Well, which one is the best?" asks River.

"It says here *desafiadora* means defiant, or standing up for yourself. Or *dinámico*. From the word dynamite. "

"Oh that's perfect. *Dinámico*," says River.

"*Diablo* Dinora is better," shouts Danita.

"Shut up, crybaby. *Chillona*." Why didn't Danita disappear instead of Papi?

"Okay," says River. "Mr. Hawaii calls you Diva Dee. I'm calling you Dina Dee. Short for *Dinámica*."

"Funny."

"I'm serious. Dina Dee. You're daring and gutsy, standing up for yourself that way."

I swallow an uh-oh down into my stomach remembering what I said about River.

Before River goes home he says, "When in doubt, be dynamic, okay, Dina Dee?"

"You're weird," I tell him as I close the door.

I wander into Danita's room. "What do people do at a sleepover?" I ask very casually.

"Aw, poor widdle DeeDee wants us to help her," says Danita.

"Never mind," I say.

"She's kidding," says Andrea. "Of course we'll help you. But it's been a while since fourth grade, so things might have changed."

"Dancing, maybe that video game. I forgot the name. You're good at that," says Danita.

"Dance Forever," I say. I do love dancing. But am I still too pudgy? I wonder. Will they make fun of me?

"And snacks. Sometimes truth or dare," says Andrea.

"Makeup," offers Danita. "I've got some you can have."

"And stories. Scary stories. Funny stories. Remember that scary story about the man with the hook?" Danita and Andrea scream at the same time and then giggle.

While Danita digs around in her makeup drawer, Andrea tells me the story so I can tell it at the sleepover. Then Danita makes me a prop to use with the story.

"Put it in your blanket before you start telling it. It's better that way," she says as she tries to catch my twitching eyelashes with her mascara brush.

I don't think I'm going to be very good at this whole sleepover thing. Maybe I should just forget about it. Why do I even want to spend the night with Noodle-nose Nancy and her sidekick Sherie? They make me feel like one of those leftover crayons that won't fit back in the box. Then I smile, remembering what River called me. My new nickname. Dina Dee. A little pepita of determination starts to grow in my heart. Bring it on. There's no stopping Dina Dee.

CHAPTER TWELVE

D IS FOR DINA DEE

"Carbs," says Sherie, and she makes a nasty face at her sandwich. She pulls the meat off and stuffs the bread back into one of the four compartments on a plastic box. She opens a second compartment and eats a Dorito.

We're at lunch detention on Friday. In the quiet and cushy conference room so the lunch supervisors can keep an eye on us. Not a huge punishment, if you ask me.

I don't say anything to Sherie, but Doritos are carbs too, and probably way worse than wheat bread. I wish I didn't know these things now. I really used to love Doritos before D for Diabetes.

Nancy carefully extracts her food from a box with dividers, the same as Sherie's. "Have you ever seen a bento box?" she asks.

"No," I say. And before I can stop myself I say, "I've seen a bent toe, though."

"Is that a joke?" Nancy asks. "Oh my gawd. Sherie, did you hear that? So funny."

I swallow my smile, and pretend to concentrate on my school lunch.

I'm not supposed to drink chocolate milk, or eat pancakes and syrup, but when you're in detention they deliver the lunches instead of allowing troublemakers to stand in the lunch line. And I guess they never checked my menu choices. I'm supposed to eat the chef's salad and the chicken sandwich. I don't want to make a big deal about it, especially in front of my two new "pals," as Principal Sorry called us when she escorted us to the office. "I hope this will be the beginning of you gals becoming pals," she said. I almost barfed.

"That syrup smells soooo good. Are you going to eat all those pancakes?" Nancy eats dainty bits of food from each compartment. Instead of a plastic water bottle, she drinks flavored fizzy water from a metal can.

"I love the smell of your fizzy water," I tell her. "Are you going to eat every grain of that rice?" I can't help myself. I'm being daring. River would be so proud of me.

Sherie makes a snort, as though she's trying not to laugh but can't help herself.

"And, are you saving that bread for an art project?" I take Sherie's bread from Sherie's box and pretend I'm making pottery.

Then they both laugh. For real. Laugh out loud. Because I'm funny.

And then we talk. Really talk. About the sleepover and how Nancy's mom is going to order pizza from the most expensive pizza place. And Nancy asks if I can eat pizza, and if I can't what can her mom make for me? I ask if she has the Dance Forever game and she has the latest version, so that's going to be great, if I can stop worrying about being a gordita.

Sherie makes us promise not to laugh if she brings her Snufflebunny and we laugh right then, right in her face. I have a tight squeezy pinch in my stomach, which might be nerves, or joy, or maybe the three pancakes.

"So, DeeDee," says Nancy as she clicks the covers closed on the compartments of her bento box. "How does your neighbor even eat without fingers?"

Pinch. That spot in my stomach again. I put my hand over the spot. I remember the first time River ate with me in the hospital. I remember how I stared at him. Now, it's not weird. It's just the way River is.

Why is Noodlenose so curious about River? I hate it. I don't know how to answer her. I roll my hands together the way River does. It's hard to breathe. As if taking a breath would break my lungs. I want to be Dina Dee. But they're waiting for me to say something funny. And they just started to like me. And River has lots of friends.

I make my hands into lobster claws. "Chop, chop. Chopsticks," I say.

My two new friends copy me. "Chop, chop. Chopsticks," they shriek. And they laugh.

Pinch goes my stomach.

•

It's not only my stomach that goes pinch when Mrs. Marsh checks me after lunch.

"Oh, DeeDee, you know better," she tut-tuts when I list the food I ate. I have to pee on a little strip and drink a bottle of water.

I wander back to class. River sticks a note in my hand when I walk by his desk. "Library postponed," it says. Not again. He always has things to do.

•

My phone is for emergencies. That's what Mami says. But what kind of emergency? I text River on Saturday:

Emergency. WRKing on Papi's LTR. Need string cheese.

He texts back. **Come over and dance for it, Dina Dee.**

On Sunday I text River. **Emergency. 50 degrees. Try-outs soon. Sk8BRD?**

River texts back. **I'm at church.**

Fudge buckets. I forgot. I go practice by myself in the speed-bump parking lot.

•

On Monday my language arts group goes really well. We just started reading TOD, *Tale of Despereaux*. Which I pronounce des-per-row, thanks to Yari and her French lessons. Her pom-pom is in the bottom of my book bag and I'm planning to put it back. It's okay that she likes River more than me. I like River more than me, too. And he'll be a good SLT member. This have a friend, be a friend thing really makes me think a lot.

So, back to TOD. It's another book with an animal main character. A mouse. And he saves the princess. Mrs. Cruella wants us to compare the characters' motivation in all the books we've studied.

Sherie says, "I'm motivated by shopping."

Nancy laughs. "Me too. So is that money?"

Samantha says, "No, that's greed. But none of the characters were greedy."

Nicole says, "What about fear? Ragweed was afraid of the cat. Annemarie was afraid her best friend Ellen would be sent away in *Number the Stars*."

Sherie adds, "And Despereaux is afraid the rats will hurt the princess."

"Okay," says Nancy. "Let's write those down." Then she almost makes me wet my pants when she looks at me and says. "What do you think, DeeDee?"

"What about love? All the characters were scared, but if they didn't love their family or their friends, would they bother to risk their lives?" I almost make myself wet my pants when I say this. It sounds smart, doesn't it? Not like something Dopey DeeDee would come up with.

Everyone stares at me like I've sprouted another head. I bite my lip. Maybe it's not smart. Maybe it's really stupid.

Nancy opens the marker. "That's really good, DeeDee. I bet that's exactly what Mrs. Krewell wanted us to figure out."

I think about what River said about Nancy's family, moving into this neighborhood. The first Asian family. I bet her parents were scared, but they loved their family and were more scared about not sending their kids to a good school. I think about Nancy with such an important brother.

I think about Mami. How scared she must be about my diabetes without Papi or our trailer. But she keeps working hard and doing everything she can. Because she loves us. Then I think about me. I guess I am sort of greedy. Worrying about myself and wanting everything.

And I'm afraid of so many things. Danny leaving again. Papi never coming home. Ending up in the hospital. But I do love my family. That's why I want to find Papi. For Mami. For Danita. For Danny. So everything will go back to normal.

We're so busy writing and drawing we hardly notice when Mrs. Cruella stops to check on our progress. "Oh, this is exceptional. Great job."

Nancy points at me. "It was DeeDee's idea."

Talk about almost wetting my pants.

After lunch River's reading group goes to the reading corner. Lucky. They chose their own book to read. Nancy says something to River. His cheeks get rosy and his eyes get wet. He rolls his hands. I almost rush over and punch her, but thinking about the sleepover stops me. Instead I just slip next door to join the reading dummies.

•

When I get home after school, I eat a snack. A healthy one. By The Way. Apples and peanut butter. It's no fun missing art to go get tested every hour—so from now on, no cheating.

Ever since Mami gave me a phone River always texts me when he gets home from school. He walks with Colin and it takes him a little longer. Today I wait fifteen minutes. No text. Finally I text him.

RU home yet?
Yes, one minute.

Danita and Andrea are making a playlist for the *quinceañera*. In between "Single Ladies" and "Cha-Cha Slide" they're sprinkling in Mexican songs, and some waltzes, "*El Jarabe Tapatio*," and "*El Vals De Las Mariposas*." That pinchy place in my stomach does its squeezy thing when I hear that song. That's the song Papi is supposed to dance with Danita. I still haven't sent the letters for Papi and we haven't gone to his work, either. If we don't find him, Danny will have to do the Father-Daughter dance. Unless he's at his NGYPC training. And that will be sad, won't it?

It's not one minute before River comes over. It's more like twenty minutes and when I open the door, before he even acknowledges me, his text alert vibrates and he checks his phone. Then he does some fast texting, ignoring me the whole time. Finally, he shuts off his phone.

"Ah, don't mind me, I'm just part of the furniture," I say.

"That was an important text."

"Fine," I say.

"What's eating you?"

"What's eating you?"

He says something under his breath. It sounds like, you can't have your cake, but it might be I don't live in a cave. I guess both make sense.

"So, who was it?"

"Yari."

A little steam comes out of my ears, but I breathe deeply. River and I can be friends. River and Yari can be friends. *Mi casa, tu casa.* Whoops. No Spanish. My house, your house.

"Here," I say. "I finished translating the letter. And I added my phone number."

"Fine. I will email it tomorrow and print the copies to mail. You'll have to pay me back for the stamps." He sounds very business-y

"Want to go to the library tomorrow?"

River doesn't answer. "What's that music?"

"The *quinceañera* play list."

"Danita," he calls.

"*Hola, Río,*" says Danita.

"*Hola chica,*" says River.

"Oh My Gatos," I say, rolling my eyes. Really? She calls him *Río*? River in Spanish?

River pulls a huge bag of balloons from his backpack in all shades of blue. "Here, these were leftover from a fundraiser at my mom's work."

"Perfect," says Danita.

"And she says to tell you the owner of a print shop she knows owes her a favor, so once you finish your invitation design, send her the file."

"What's going on?" I ask.

"Danita invited my mom and me to the *quinceañera*."

"I'll send you an official invite once they're done," says Danita. "*Gracias, Río*."

She takes the balloons, puts them in the box marked QUINCEAÑERA, and goes back to Andrea and the playlist.

"I gotta go," says River.

"But you just got here."

"Chop, chop," says River, and he glares at me. Then he closes the door. Hard.

So Noodlenose told him what I said during lunch detention. I swallow a big gulp of uh-oh. And my stomach squeezes. Hard.

I text River, **I'm sorry. I didn't mean it.**

Are you embarrassed to be my friend at school?

No. I promise. I'll try harder. Library tomorrow?

It's a long time before River responds. **OK.**

•

All day at school I try to be River's friend. I try to catch his eye when I come in the classroom after my visit to Mrs. Marsh, but he never looks at me. I try to casually walk by his desk on my way to turn in my homework, but he and Colin are studying a picture in a book. And at recess I stay off the jungle gym and walk around in the rubber mulch watching the soccer scrimmage.

River stays on the far side of the field blasting the ball into the net every time they pass to him.

When the recess bell rings, I try to get in line near River, but he offers to pick up the soccer cones for Bull-Face since it's starting to drizzle. Bull-Face smiles at him. I walk by the special-needs lunch table, planning to mention today's "library" trip or say good job on the soccer field, but Yari swoops in front of me.

"Brandon loves the idea," she says to River. "But can you meet after school? To make it work we have to start it by March first."

No, I want to say, he can't. Not today, but I don't. I'm sure River will tell her.

When I get home from school I tell Danita that River and I are going to the library.

"When you get back, go to River's. Andrea and I have orientation," she says.

"What does that mean?" I ask.

"Gawd. Don't you know anything?" Danita says. "It's so you know about high school."

My text alert goes off. I grab my jacket and the key. In my pocket I have the little coin purse with $23.67 in it. I get to the hall and open my text messages.

Emergency meeting after school. Postpone library.

I feel like the end of a video game when you lose. Tiny dying fireworks. Fading music. Game Over.

Now what? Nobody needs me. Not Papi. Not River. Not Danita. Not Danny. Not Yari. Not Mami. Well, maybe Mami still needs me. And we all need Papi.

I take a deep breath. I don't need anybody to help me. I'm Dina Dee. I can do it by myself. How hard can it be? I walk to the bus stop. I take the map from my pocket. When Bus 29 pulls up, I get on. It's the same bus driver from my trips with Mami to La Paloma, her favorite Mexican grocery store. He eyes me suspiciously. I nod at him and plop into a seat.

Mister, I'm on detective business. Wait until the receptionist gives me the address of Papi's big new house in Mexico. Wait until I see Mr. Villapando in the parking lot and he tells me Papi got a new better job in Mexico. Wait until I tell River I figured it out. By myself.

When the sign in the front of the bus flashes AVON STREET, I pull the cord and get off. I think I need Bus 76 now. I check the map. No. I need Bus 67. And I'm not sure which direction I need to go. I wait. And wait. My hands get cold. I put them in my pocket. I feel my phone and the little pink coin purse. Why did I steal that anyway? Do people know I take stuff? Nobody wants a friend who takes stuff.

Bus 67 rumbles up. I hop up the steps. "Excuse me," I say. "Does this bus go to North Avenue?"

"Other side," growls the bus driver and I get off. Before I can cross the street, I see Bus 67 fly past going the other way. Oh no. I trudge across the street and wait some more.

Is this how Mami feels waiting for a bus everyday? Why doesn't she get her driver's license? Did she learn to drive in Mexico? I know she was twenty years old, and already married to Papi when she moved here. Why didn't Papi help Mami get her driver's license?

Bus 67 finally comes. I squeeze into the only seat left on the bus. A high school boy and girl in front of me are very kissy-facey. Gross. I look away and watch the sign until it flashes NORTH AVENUE. I get off. Which way do I walk? I close my eyes. I imagine Papi and me driving to TAICO to pick up his check. Parking at a big white building with windows that reflect the sun like aluminum foil. Cashing his check. Getting gas. Buying me a blue raspberry Slurpee. Pulling through the car wash.

I open my eyes. Way down the street I see a sign—a big green flower under the letters BP. A gas station. And when I finally walk up the sidewalk, I get that little pitter-patter in my heart when I think of Papi. I'm so close to knowing where he is I can almost see him. I open the jingly door and get myself a blue raspberry Slurpee.

I stand on my tiptoes to put a dollar on the counter. "Excuse me," I ask the cashier. "Could you tell me which way to TAICO?" I take a big slurp of my Slurpee.

The woman in line behind me leans forward. "TAICO? Hadn't you heard? They shut down two weeks back." Her cigarette breath stays in the air between us.

I stumble toward the door with my Slurpee. My hands freezing. My heart cold.

"Hey, it's a dollar-twenty-seven," calls the cashier.

I push open the door. The BP is blurry. The flower is blurry. Everything is blurry. I set my Slurpee down on the sidewalk and wipe my eyes with my sleeve. I lean against the wall and suck my Slurpee until the brain freeze stops my tears. I toss the rest of it in the trash. TAICO shut down? What happened to all the people? What happened to Mr. Villapando?

I lift my 500-pound feet and plod back to the bus stop. My stomach lurches and I wish I'd eaten a snack. While my pepita of hope slips away, so does the daylight. At the bus stop, the streetlight on the corner flickers, like it wants to shine but is afraid it's too early. And maybe afraid the other streetlights will make fun of her. "Look at Flashy Flora, always showing off. She can't even shine. Who does she think she is?"

I must be loopy. Talking street lights? I board the bus and lay my head against the window. Did Papi leave us on purpose? Or was River right about Papi being undocumented? Maybe Papi got deported. Or worse. What if he's—NO. I refuse to say that word.

My brain hurts from thinking. My stomach aches from blue raspberry Slurpee. And my feet hurt from walking. I close my eyes.

I jolt awake when someone jiggles my arm. "Little miss, this is the last stop. You want to transfer, you got to get off."

"Did we pass Avon Street?"

"We sure did," says the bus driver. "You can catch another sixty-seven bus going back that way in about thirty minutes."

I stand up and know I'm in trouble. My heart pounds. The floor spins while I struggle to focus. I'm shaky and hold onto the door for balance as I step down from the bus. I take tiny steps to the bus stop bench and lower myself to sit. I'm so thirsty. Where am I? I pull my phone from my pocket. My hands are sweaty. Four text messages from Danita. I squint at my phone.

What time will you be home? 4:32 PM

You better answer me. 4:45 PM

I have to leave. Get your butt home. 5:15 PM

If you don't text me back in ten minutes I'm calling Mami. 5:30 PM

I check the time. 5:35. Oh Land O'Lakes. My head hurts so bad. But Danita will think I'm such a baby if I tell her I'm lost.

My phone rings. Danita. "Hello?" I say.

"DeeDee? Where are you? I'm going to be late for my orientation."

"Just go. I'll text River and tell him I'm going to be a late coming to his house."

The minute I hear myself I know I made a mistake.

"River? You told me you and River went to the library! Mami will kill me. You have to ruin everything, don't you?"

"I'm sorry, Danita." I start to cry. And I hate crying. A taxi honks.

"What's that noise? DeeDee? Are you okay? Where are you?"

I snuffle into the phone. "I don't know. I fell asleep on the bus."

Danita says a swear word which I won't repeat. "Well, look at the street signs. Look at the buildings. What do you see?"

"I'm on North Avenue. And the sign across the street says Downy Place."

"Downy and North? You're at the library, you tonto." Danita laughs into the phone.

I look behind me. Northlake Public Library. The library? I'm not that far away. "Danita, I don't feel good."

"I'm calling Danny. He'll be there in ten minutes."

I hear the worry in Danita's voice. "Tell him to bring me a juice and a snack."

"Don't worry, *Mija*, don't worry."

"Danita?" If Papi can't be at the *quinceañera*, then she needs me. She needs us. Her family.

"What *reinita*?"

"I want to be in your *quinceañera*. Is it too late?" Why did I ever act so mean and awful?

Danita laughs. "Oh *mija*, of course you can."

•

When Mami gets home she thinks we should go to the hospital. My blood sugar is still really low. But I didn't pass out. And I'm not shaky anymore. Mami wants to know what happened. Danita stares at me. Danny stares at me.

"River and I were supposed to go to the library, but he had a meeting so I tried to go by myself. And I forgot to eat my snack."

Danita raises her eyebrows. Danny shakes his head. They know I'm not telling the truth, but they don't know what the truth is.

Mami points at us. "*Sin valores*," she hisses.

I feel about one quarter inch tall.

"Grounded," Mami tells me and humphs on her way to the kitchen.

"But the sleepover is Friday. Can I go, please?" I beg.

"Two days grounded," she calls with her head in the fridge, figuring out dinner.

"I'm sorry about your orientation," I say to Danita.

"I'll go tomorrow. I was supposed to meet some-body there tonight, but it's okay."

"Somebody special?" I ask and make a kissing noise.

"Oh, shut up, DeeDee," says Danita, and she gets red in the face.

•

I'm grounded on Wednesday and on Thursday when River goes with Danny to the high school to register for the special training program. When they return, River comes over.

"Danny says you almost had to go to the hospital," says River. "What happened?"

"I went to the library by myself." I have to use our code word because Danita's in her bedroom and Danny hasn't left for night school.

"Oh, no. You did? I'm sorry I stayed for SLT instead of keeping our plan."

And he looks so sorry I have to believe him. I whisper, "They closed the plant."

"No!" says River. "That's terrible. And listen, DeeDee. I really am sorry. If something happened to you . . . well, I wasn't being a good friend to ditch you like that. It's just that, well," River's hands are rolling and his eyes flit around the room. "Um, it bugs me when you care more about what other people think than what I think."

"I don't," I say, softly.

"And I don't want you to be my friend because you feel sorry for me. Because I'm different. Like some kids at school do."

"I don't," I say again, louder.

"Or think you're great like they do for being nice to me and showing me favoritism because I have a disability."

"Oh-Em-Gee. I don't," I yell.

River jumps. "Sometimes I don't know if you really want to be friends with me."

I fold my arms across my stomach so it won't pinch and squeeze me. How do I say that it's me, not him, that's the problem? How do I say that I'm not Dina Dee and not Diva Dee, but Down-in-the-Dumps Dee?

"I do," is all I say. "I do. I just mess up."

"As long as you learn from your mess-ups," says River.

Danny walks into the living room. In a deep voice River says, "Why do we fall, Bruce?"

Danny says, "So we can learn to pick ourselves up."

"Batman?" I ask.

"Right, you are," says River in a Yoda voice.

"Leave, I must," says Danny and sits down to tie his shoes.

"Weird, you are," I say and they both laugh.

"Want to go to the skatepark on Saturday if it's nice? My mom has an errand over there, so she said she'll drop us off if Danny can pick us up."

"The skatepark?" I ask. "Does a bear poop in the woods? Danny, can you? Mrs. Wang is dropping me off Saturday morning at eight."

River rolls his eyes. "Oh. The sleepover. I can't believe you're still going to that." River starts to calculate in his head. "So if we go at nine, can you pick us up around noon, or do you have National Guard?"

"Nope," says Danny. "I'll be there."

"Awesome saucesome," I say. I'm glad River's not mad anymore. And I'm glad I can learn from my mistakes.

River gives us the salute and goes home.

"Maybe I'll text Freddie," says Danny. "He used to hang out there all the time."

"Do you still have his number? I thought you weren't friends anymore," I say.

"I haven't talked to him in a year. Maybe he's different. Maybe we're both different."

"Maybe he knows something about Papi. His uncle used to ride with Papi everyday."

Danny takes a deep breath and nods his head. "True. He used to be a good friend. *Amistades verdaderas, mantienen las puertas abiertas.* Always keep your door open for a true friend. Did you know it's a song?" says Danny. "Want me to sing it?"

Danny can't sing. And I mean, really can't sing. "Does a bear poop in the house?" I say, and he laughs.

CHAPTER THIRTEEN

D IS FOR DISASTER

The sleepover starts at six tonight. I have pins and needles poking me all over. And I feel like a window blind. One minute I'm open and brightly excited and the next I'm dark and moody and want to stay home. River pops by after school and still thinks I'm highly illogical for even wanting to go.

Danita puts on her playlist to get my mind off things. She teaches River a few more dance steps for one of the ballads. Not "*El Vals De La Mariposa.*" That's the one Danny might have to do for Papi.

"Come on, DeeDee," says Danny. "Let's show these two how it's done."

When the song ends, both River and Danny clap. "Gordita, you're really a good dancer. Why don't you dance instead of skateboard for that Spring Thing at your school?" Danny asks.

"Yah," says River. "You'll get my vote."

I hit my head with my hand. "You guys don't know anything. They'll never pick me. They only choose the best from each grade."

"But you could do these dances. Nobody knows how to do these dances."

"You should do it," says Daniel. "If you do it, I'll come."

"You won't have to. They won't pick me."

"Well, you should try," say Danny and River, at the exact same time.

I go pack. And unpack. Then pack again. I pack two pairs of underwear. Then I add three more, just in case. I pack my stretchy yoga pants and a T-shirt to sleep in. All my other pajamas are disgusting. Except for the princess ones, and remember, they're too babyish. Danita tries to help. She puts outfits together. I shake my head. I put outfits together. She shakes her head.

"DeeDee, OMG. Your belly. You can't wear that belly shirt!" Danita tells me.

"I like this shirt."

"Here, wear my Fashion Fifteen shirt." She hands me a shirt that looks as transparent as bread wrapping.

"Everything will show!" I hold it up to my chest.

"You have to wear a cami, silly," she says and throws me a strappy little shirt.

I put it on and suck in my belly.

"That's cute," Danita says.

"DeeDee," calls Mami. "Danny is waiting."

At the last minute I grab my teddy bear and stuff it down, down, down deep in my bag. I will only get it out if I have to. I put my new-to-me cell phone in my pocket.

Mami kisses me. "Do you have things for your diabetes?"

Mami can't remember the names and I'm tired of telling her. Lancing device. Glucometer. "Yes," is all I say.

"Daniel will bring me to the house," she says. "Midnight. Remember. To check you."

Did I mention that in the middle of every night Mami checks my blood sugar? I used to wake up, but now I sleep right through it. I'm horrified that Mami has to come to the sleepover. I begged to set an alarm and do it myself. She says Nancy's mom promised not to tell the girls. But can I trust Nancy's mom? I don't know.

Danny is good at directions. He finds Nancy's house right away. He parks in front. I get out. He gets out.

"What're you doing?"

"Walking you to the door."

"Why?"

"It's what guys are supposed to do."

I giggle. He carries my bag. I carry my rolled-up quilt.

"Are you sure about this?"

I'm so nervous, I only manage to giggle again. I tell myself I'm Dina Dee.

"If you want to come home, call my cell phone."

"What if you're sleeping?"

"Call. No matter what."

It's the biggest house I've ever seen. The garage is attached to the house.

"They must be rich," I whisper.

"Or loaded with debt," Danny whispers back.

"What's debt?"

"Never mind."

The door opens. Nancy and Sherie gawk at Danny. Their mouths hang open.

"My brother, Daniel," I say. They look ridiculous.

"I didn't know you had a brother," says Nancy after she closes the door. "Does he go to Northlake High?"

"He's so cute," says Sherie. "Does he have a girlfriend?"

See what I mean? Ridiculous.

We go downstairs to a room with a humongous TV and two big comfy couches, the kind with the pop-up foot rests. Nicole and Samantha are already lounging. I see sleeping bags spread out over the carpeting.

"We're going to sleep in the family room so we can stay up really late. Is that your sleeping bag?" Nancy asks me, in a tone that means she can't believe I brought a blanket instead.

I hate that tone. But I'm Dina Dee, so I say, "I'll have you know I take this blanket to all my sleepovers. It's haunted by the spirit of my madrina."

"Oooh. Can I sleep next to you?" Sherie moves her sleeping bag and Snufflebunny to the end and I lay out my faded, purple-and-pink plaid, haunted quilt.

I'm sure you've been to plenty of sleepovers, so you know better than me what happens. Eat. Laugh. Burp. Giggle. Eat some more. Put on movies and talk right over them. Play games and stop in the middle to do something else. Nancy's mom tries hard to push the carrots and cheese sticks and I'm polite, but I eat plenty of Doritos, too. The kind from the purple bag. Spicy Sweet Chili. I'm in love with those and you know Mami doesn't buy them anymore.

I eat a handful or two of M&Ms. Sneaky, so nobody sees. Oh, and five pieces of pizza. Nicole eats six, but then she barfs. We keep the lights out when we dance. Turns out I'm very good at Dance Forever Nation and I get the highest score, plus add my name to the top challengers, and even though I feel sort of foggy and tired, I'm having a great time.

Everybody puts on their pj's. Nancy and Sherie have matching silky robes outlined with white fur, but I feel okay in my yoga pants and T-shirt after I see Nicole's pink, ruffly, babyish nightgown and Samantha's stretched-out, faded pj bottoms. We wiggle into our floor beds.

"I've got a ghost story," Nancy says in a fake spooky voice. "Ready, everybody?

She tells a stupid story about a ghost dripping blood, ending with a man saying, 'Hey, you need a Band-Aid.' Then she laughs, a seal-bark laugh, over and over. I don't laugh. It's not even funny. Nancy is getting on my nerves, more than ever.

"I've got a scary one." I make my voice low and shaky. I tell the story about the hook murderer that Danita and Andrea taught me. Just before the story ends I ask, "Guess what's attached to the car door handle?" I wait for dramatic effect.

"THE HOOK!" I reach into my blanket, pull out the hanger that Danita and Andrea made into a hook, and poke Nancy's arm with it.

Everyone grabs onto everybody else and screams. Loud. The way I imagine a pig squeals when they're turning him into bacon.

"Oh My Gosh. That was soooooo good!" Nicole says.

"That gives me an idea," says Nancy. "Let's play Boyfriend."

Sherie groans but Nancy keeps talking.

Sherie whispers to me, "She always wants to play Boyfriend. She's boy crazy."

"I don't know how to play," I whisper back. My head is aching and I just want to go to sleep. I pull my teddy bear from my bag and hold him tight.

"You'll see."

It turns out to be the stupidest game I've ever played. You have to make up a sentence using a boy's name and the words on the dice. I go last and Nancy chooses River for my boyfriend. She might be the most annoying person I've ever met.

By the time Boyfriend is over, I feel super tired.

"Are you okay?" Sherie nudges me.

I'm very foggy. My brain is spongy. Remember. Remember. Remember. I sit up. My glucometer. I forgot to check. "What time is it?"

Nancy answers, "Almost the witching hour. Midnight."

I pull my kit from my bag and, in the dark, I feel my way to the bathroom. I flip on the light. Cerulean wallpaper with orange paper lanterns and long black boats swims over me. Silver lamps with white shades balance on the sides of a silver mirror. Thin, whiter-than-white towels hang on polished silver racks and the way they're folded makes me think they aren't for wiping sweaty faces.

I open the cabinet and find a tissue box. I'm shaky. Woozy. And so thirsty. I sit on the toilet and dab my face with tissues. I use at least twenty. I know my number will be high even before I check. And it is. Off the charts. Everybody is busy giggling hysterically as I tiptoe up the stairs.

"Oh, I was coming down to get you," says Nancy's mom.

"You have a nice bathroom," I tell her.

"I enjoy playing at interior decorating."

I never knew anyone who did that before. Interior decorating. I might really like that. Putting colors together.

"Oh, Dinora. *Mija!*" Mami says as I walk into the living room.

I whisper the number to her then sit down. Mami does the math to be sure she gives me enough insulin. I will not pass out in Nancy's living room. No I will not.

"She need water."

Mrs. Wang rushes off and brings back a glass of water. I slurp and rub my eyes. Oh My Gatos. Why did I eat all that pizza? Mami taps the syringe and pulls up my T-shirt. "*Porque no llevaste pijamas?*"

I don't tell her why I'm not wearing pajamas. Mami thinks everything is a blessing. Every bag of used clothes. Every bargain at the thrift store. She doesn't understand being fashionable. We wait, my head in Mami's lap. Mrs. Wang standing statue-still, in her swooshy pajamas and fleecy robe, not one hair out of place. She doesn't know what to say.

"What color is it?" I ask Nancy's mom, still thinking about the bathroom.

"What color?" She's confused. "Oh, the bathroom? Teal. Done in the chinoiserie style."

The word sounds so rich to me. I try to repeat it. "Cheenwasorry?"

Nancy's mom laughs. "Almost. Chinoiserie. It means in the old Chinese style."

Then Mami checks me again. "Need to check again. Maybe need more. *Te quieres ir?*"

"No, don't make me leave, Mami. Please. I'll check, I promise."

"I can set my alarm," says Mrs. Wang.

Mami pushes herself off the couch and leans against the doorpost to put her shoes on. She seems very squatty and worn-out next to sleek and stylish Mrs. Wang. Like old sneakers next to brand new Nikes. Old sneakers that work hard all day and can't even rest at night.

I wonder if Mami feels out of place here. With her English that needs work. The same as me. With my broken insulin regulator. Coming from our too-many-people-and-too-few-beds apartment to this too-many-rooms-and-too-few-people house. I don't know, I decide. Maybe grownups learn to fit in, no matter where they go. Maybe they just accept that everyone's different and they're okay with it. I jump up and hug Mami tight.

"*Te quiero*, I love you," she breathes into my hair.

"*Te quiero más*, I love you more," I breathe back.

"DeeDee! What are you doing?" Nancy is on the top of the steps. "We're playing truth or dare. Come on."

My heart drops lower than my insulin, but I'm Dina Dee. "It's a real nice bathroom." I tell Nancy's mom on my way past her. "Cerulean I think. A cross between Indigo and Aquamarine." Mrs. Wang stares at me and I follow Nancy downstairs.

"Why—" Nancy starts to ask but I bounce in front of her and catapult into the mess of sleeping bags, knocking Sherie over.

"Your turn," Sherie tells me.

"Truth," I say. My nose wrinkles remembering the coffee grounds from playing this game with Danita and Andrea.

I know they've already decided what truth they want me to tell. Nancy blurts it out fast. "You have to tell us a secret about River."

My heart stops. Why can't they just leave him alone? What has he ever done to them? I rack my brain for a secret that River wouldn't mind me telling. Definitely not about his toes. I promised him.

"What's the dare?" I feel panicked. Like a lamb trapped by wolves.

"You have to call River," says Sherie. "And we need to hear his voice."

My brain is whirling. Maybe River's mom will answer. But I know she won't. Maybe River won't answer. But I know he will. He told me he sets his phone on vibrate and keeps it under his pillow for emergencies. And he'll worry that I'm calling in the middle of the night. He'll worry about me. He'll worry because he's my friend.

You know that green feeling just before you throw up? Well that's the feeling in my stomach while I lie on the itchy rug in my haunted quilt, wishing I could go home and knowing I'm too chicken.

"I have to pee first," I say and streak into the bathroom still carrying my diabetes kit. I pull out my phone and text Danny.

Me: **Are you awake?**

Why?

I need help.

I'm coming to get you.

Me: **No. Not that kind of help.**

What?

Can you pretend to be River's voice? In a minute.

I quickly create a new contact with Danny's number and River's name and delete Danny's old contact, the way River showed me.

I flush the toilet and wash my hands with the fluffy-foamy soap, but I let my hands drip-dry as I head back to the family room.

"What took so long?" Nancy asks. "Did you decide? Truth or dare?"

"Dare." I punch the number and put it on speaker. Ring. Ring.

"It's okay." Nicole reassures me. "He's probably got his phone on silent."

Ring. Ring.

"Then you'll have to tell us a truth," taunts Nancy.

"Hello." I hear a familiar voice, but it's not Danny. Ah-ha! It's Danita. Danny is so smart. He figured out they would recognize his deep voice. I close my eyes and take a deep breath. Everything will be okay. I can keep my promise to River and hold my own with the wolves.

"Hello?" Danita says again. "Who is this? DeeDee?"

"Okay?" I hold the phone up and show River's contact picture.

"Hey," says Nancy. She points at the number under River's name. "That's not River's number. I looked in your contacts before. You tricked us." She flashes her phone in my face. "I'm calling your boyfriend."

"No. Stop it." I lunge for her phone and she swings her arm away from me. I grab the fur on the edge of her silky robe to pull her closer and there's a ripping sound.

"You ripped my robe," Nancy screams.

"Hang up!" I scream back. "I'll tell a truth."

"You don't have to, DeeDee," says Samantha, in a surprisingly loud voice. "It's okay."

"Everybody knows you're a liar." Nancy scoots away from me, stroking the fur on the ripped edge of her robe as if it's a kitten. "Your whole illegal immigrant family lies."

Suddenly it's quiet. Quiet like the doctor's office. Quiet like the library. Quiet like waiting for a firecracker to explode.

I stand up, and squeeze my fingernails into my palms. Here's what I'm thinking: I hate you. All of you. But you will not beat me. All their eyes stare at me, like I've bewitched them.

"Oh yah? You don't know anything about my family. We're just as legal as you. And here's your truth. River has four toes. That's it. Four toes. They put his big toe for his thumb. And he's my neighbor. Not my friend. Just my neighbor. That's all. Happy now?"

Then from another world away we hear a faint voice. "DeeDee. What's happening? Who's there? DeeDee, can you hear me?"

I lift up sleeping bags until I see the screen of my phone. River's face smiles up at me but Danita's voice squeaks questions from the speaker. I stare at Nancy, burning her with my hate.

"Tell Danny to pick me up," I scream into the phone. "Now."

CHAPTER FOURTEEN

D IS FOR DEAF

Nicole helps me roll up my blanket. Sherie pats Nancy's back. Samantha tells me to stay, but I don't answer. Mrs. Wang wants to know what's wrong. When I see Danny's car I run outside and jump in. I take deep breaths, like I've been underwater and just came up to the surface.

"What happened?" Danny asks, and I tell him the whole story.

"It's hard to fit in sometimes," he says. "I dropped out to because it was just easier to be with the drop-out group. But it was like Papi said about the wolves. It's not worth trying to be accepted by some groups."

Danny steers with one hand. His tattoo peeks from the cuff of his jacket, just the swirls and the tip of the arrow, as if the arrow is trying to escape. At the stoplight, he puts his arm around me. I see two little lines between his eyebrows. Worry lines. His face—half dark and half light in the night reflection. His eyes—both sad and kind.

"DeeDee, maybe truth or dare can teach us both a lesson. Accept who we are and dare to stand up for ourselves and not trade the truth for other people, no matter what. Before it's too late. Before we lose good friends and disappoint people who love us."

"Like River and Papi?"

"Yah, like River and Papi," he says and the light turns green. "But I think River will forgive you."

"And so will Papi," I say, but in a whisper. "So will Papi."

•

When I wake up Saturday, it's a perfect day outside. My crayons would make it a Granny-Smith-Apple day combined with a Periwinkle sky. But inside my head it's a gray day. A drizzly day. A mummy-tomb day. I should be worried about checking my levels after my eating binge last night, but I'm more preoccupied with my sleepover fiasco. Replaying everything that happened. I should have listened to River. What do I care that

Nancy likes me? Why do I want to be friends with girls who make fun of people?

I wait for River to pick me up at nine o'clock while I eat a healthy breakfast. Then I wait some more. I pack some snacks. And watch TV. And wait some more. It's past nine-thirty, but everyone here is still sleeping. I guess Mami and Danny had late nights because of me. Is River still sleeping? Is his mom still sleeping? Where is he?

I call his number. "Hi, you've reached River the Geek. Leave it at the beep." I smile hearing he stole the funny answering message I created and put it on his phone.

I wait thirty more minutes and quietly open my door and walk down to River's apartment. I press my ear to his door. I hear music, so I knock.

"Why DeeDee, I thought you were at a sleepover." Mrs. Ramos-Henry looks confused. She doesn't invite me in.

"I was. Last night. But River said he'd pick me up at nine to go to the skatepark."

Mrs. Ramos-Henry stands very still and stares at me around the door at me. Finally she asks, "Did something happen between you and River?"

"No."

"I took him to the skatepark already. He said you didn't want to go with him because you were at a sleepover. I'm sorry." And she shuts the door.

What? What? What? I don't understand. What happened? I get my phone out of my pocket. He must have called me. Left me a message. Something must be wrong with my phone. Maybe it was off. Maybe I accidentally messed it up. Maybe I erased it. I frantically press buttons, trying to find missed phone calls.

Nothing.

I race back to my apartment and knock on Danny's door.

"What?" Danny growls. "I'm sleeping."

"I need a ride. It's important."

"I'm in bed, DeeDee."

"But I missed my ride to the skatepark. I have to go. I have to."

The door opens. Danny stands there in his boxers, his hair shaggy and his eyes baggy. He blinks at me.

"I'm sorry. I don't know what happened. I think I missed River's call. But I've got to go. Especially, now. *Para mantener las puertas abiertas*, to keep the door open, you know."

Danny understands. He walks into his room and pulls on jeans and a T-shirt.

He doesn't say much in the car. In fact, he doesn't say anything. When we get to the skatepark, he stares out the window like he's far away in la-la land. Is he tired? Is he thinking?

"Hey, let me out here," I say.

"Are you going to tell River what happened?" he asks when I open my door.

"No. Are you kidding? I hope he never finds out."

"Sometimes it's better to tell the truth right away," says Danny with a faraway voice that matches his faraway stare.

"Don't forget to pick us up," I say, worried he might drive right off into la-la land.

"Yah. Okay," he says, shaking himself and stretching out his arms. "I'll be here at noon or earlier if I hear back from Freddie."

"Thank you, Danny. *Te quiero.*"

I hear the whirring of skateboard wheels before I even see the skaters. I hold the tip of my board and stand at the edge of the concrete, feeling very small. Around me swirl and swoosh skaters like birds. Floating. Flying. Soaring. Twisting. Speeding. Carving. Doing tricks I can't even name. The clickety-clack of the wheels on the cement cracks drowns out the rumble of the South Shore train. The window-eyes of giant condo towers watch over the skaters.

I'm nervous about going to the skatepark. I'm not very good. What if people laugh at me?

It'll serve me right, that's what. I can't even think about River without remembering I shared his secret. I stretch my sweatshirt pockets down. Pulling it low. Over me. Shrinking me. The concrete reflects the sun, rich with sparkling diamonds, making me feel poor and ordinary. A raven-haired boy sweeps past, so close I smell his last cigarette and as he pop shoves it right in front of me, his sleeve brushes my cheek.

Whoa, he's awesome. I start looking for River. I see all sizes of boys but no girls. I skate down the ramp without running into anybody. People aren't alone here. They're in partners and groups or they have somebody watching from a bench.

I need River. I stay by the edge of the park. Slowly pushing. And then I see his curly hair. I do my best to speed down one of the middle ramps and make an impressive stop right in front of him.

I tap him. "Hey, why didn't you come get me this morning? Did I miss your call?"

He doesn't say anything, just nods at me, and motions me to follow him to a flat area on the other side of the ramps.

"We can skate back here until we're warmed up," he says.

"Hey, why didn't you pick me up?"

But River only sets his board down and pushes off, doing a wide arc and returning to me. "Okay, copy me. We'll play H-O-R-S-E, the same as basketball, but boarding."

"You're going to lose," I tell him and copy his arc perfectly.

He makes it harder and harder and I do fine until he ollies, getting about three inches of air under his board. Last time we went out he could barely get an inch.

"When did you learn that?" I ask.

"I practiced when Danny took me to the high school on Thursday."

"You know I can't do those." I pout at him.

"So? Control and timing. Push with your back foot to pop the board up and at the same time, slide your other foot to level out the board."

I try, but my board goes nowhere and I topple over backwards. I can't slide my foot at the same time as I push down.

Then River starts skating switch, swapping his back foot to the middle of the board and his front foot to the tail. He points at a kid who's taking a ramp and I watch as the kid goes up with his right foot front, but down with his left foot front. Now I get why fakie is important for ramps.

Pretty soon, I've got H-O-R-S and he only has H. Time to play hardball. I tuck my T-shirt into my jeans and run, holding onto my skateboard with two hands. I set it down and flip up into a handstand. I've never tried this before but I can do a handstand anywhere. I've even done them on the balance beam we used to have at Lincoln Elementary.

Holy jalapeño. I'm upside down and the board is moving. But not for long. I can't steer. I careen straight into the wall, bailing in the nick of time. I pick myself up, collect my board, and look back at River. He's watching a skater flying up a vert ramp, catching some air, then flipping his board as he spins before catapulting back down.

I tap him and say, with little jealous bite in my voice, "You missed my trick."

"I'm admiring his air." He nudges my skateboard. It clatters to the ground and starts rolling. "You're the only person I know who doesn't play fair in H-O-R-S-E. I can't do handstands—or did you forget?" I can't figure out his voice. Is he teasing or is he upset with me?

"Hey, Spidey," a big kid calls to River, and he does a chin-up kind of nod.

I point after him. "Friend of yours?"

"I've come here since I was seven."

"Why Spidey?"

River holds up his two-finger hand, webs me like Spiderman, and then I get it. But I don't understand. Isn't he mad about the names? Is he just pretending it doesn't bother him? How did he learn to turn it to cool and not cruel? It's as if he knows himself so well he doesn't need to hide from anybody. He isn't embarrassed to talk about superpowers and *Star Trek* or be Dopey Dinosaura's friend.

Why can't I do that? I want to skateboard for Spring Fling because everyone will think I'm cool. But I'm not very good at skateboarding. I'm good at dancing. I think about Nancy's party. I tried so hard to be Dina Dee. And it didn't matter in the end. I didn't make any friends, and I broke a promise to a true friend.

River skates a few yards away from me and up to a tall boy with light yellow, almost white hair. They start to sign to each other.

I steer clear of the other skaters and make my way over to them.

"Hey," I say when I get close, but River doesn't look at me.

I do a little spin out move with my board. I notice both River and the kid staring at me and sort of laughing. I get the feeling the kid is signing about me.

Oh no you're not. You aren't even making fun of me. I stomp over and stare at him. The kid stares back at me.

"Take a picture. It'll last longer," I say and balance my skateboard against the wall.

"This is my friend Jeremiah," says River, signing at the same time.

Jeremiah signs to me and says, "Nice to meet you," in a silly voice.

"What's his problem? Are you guys making fun of me?"

"No, DeeDee, Jeremiah's deaf. He and I went to Learning Center for the Deaf together, but he's at Joyner Middle School now."

I feel stupid. Of course. Signing, and the way he talks. I wonder if kids at Joyner make fun of him for that. "Does he know my sister?"

River asks at the same time as he motions, but I can see some of the motions are hard for him to do with his fused-together fingers. Then he translates the motions his friend is making.

"He says yes. Danita is nice but you're prettier." To Jeremiah he says, "You're a flirt." He puts his thumbs together and wiggles his fingers like butterfly wings.

Jeremiah winks at me and says something with hand motions but River looks embarrassed and doesn't translate it for me.

"What did he say?" I ask.

"Nothing," says River.

"Hey, that's not fair. Why doesn't Jeremiah have speaker things in his head, like you?"

River translates this to Jeremiah, who shakes his head, rolls his eyes, and signs back to River.

"He wants you to know being deaf is not a sickness to cure. It's his community, uh, let's see, culture, and he's proud to be a part of it."

Then Jeremiah points down at his skateboard, says, "See you." He waves to me and I watch him grind the curb.

"I don't get it. Why would anybody want to stay deaf?"

"I doubt you'd understand." River sighs like I'm so airheaded he can see through my skull.

"Okay, whatever. If you don't want to explain."

"Fine. I'll try. It's complicated. My mom had a hard choice. I'm a CI user to the Deaf community. And hard of hearing to the hearing culture. So now I don't really fit into a culture."

"But that's crazy. Why should other people care if you want to hear?"

"That's easy for you to say, but how would your family like it if you didn't want to be Mexican anymore?" There's a knife-edge tone in River's voice I've never heard before. Almost as if he's challenging me to argue so he can chop me into little bits.

"I guess they'd be sad."

"And confused and angry, if you suddenly couldn't speak or understand Spanish."

"But that's different. You can still speak sign language to your friends."

"Yah, but some of them think CI users are traitors. And nobody likes a traitor." He looks at me when he says this and my face flushes. I remember how I felt like a traitor in detention when I made fun of how he eats. And when I told his secret at the sleepover. And how Papi might be a traitor to his family.

"In fact, sometimes I just take my CI external processor off so I fit in." River holds up his hands. "These are the biggest reason I got CI. Communicating with these isn't easy."

"But you have lots of friends." I point around the skatepark.

"They're acquaintances. Not friends." River watches Jeremiah as he attempts the wall. There's no spark in River's eyes. And no grin on his face.

Wow, this CI thing must really bother him. Like my diabetes bothers me. "You have tons of friends at school. I don't speak sign language and you don't speak Spanish, but we're friends, right? What's the big deal?"

River doesn't look at me.

"Mami says, '*Con amigos como esos, no se necesitan enemigos.*' That means with bad friends you don't need enemies."

"Yah, I see that," River says under his breath.

"And why'd you leave without me this morning? Danny was mad he had to drive me."

"I didn't think you wanted to go." A storm rages in River's voice.

"Why? You know I wanted to go."

"Not after the sleepover."

"I told you I would be ready. I even came home early because I was homesick." I take a step back from River.

"That's not what I meant." River pronounces the ending letter for every word he says, which is unusual for him. "I meant after what happened at the sleepover."

In all the days I've known River, he's never lost his temper with me. Even when he told me he didn't know if I wanted to be his friend, he just looked sad. But now, there's no more dance in his eyes. Instead, they smolder, and his nostrils flare out.

"What? Nothing happened." My mouth is dry, so dry, and my heart just punched my stomach.

River pulls out his phone. "Yah? Nancy called me last night. In the middle of the night." He twirls his board and bites his lip, not looking at me. "You broke your promise. Talk about traitors."

I hang my head. A flame of shame rises up from my toes and burns all the way to my ears. Why do these things happen to me? Why didn't I listen to Danny and tell River the truth right away? "I'm sorry," I say. "I tried to do the right thing, but it didn't work and Nancy made me so mad I lost my temper." My heart punches me again, punishing me for always messing up.

"Fine." And with a screech of his wheels, he skates away from me.

I follow him. "I'm sorry, okay? Can we just forget about it?"

He doesn't look at me. "Sort of hard to forget."

"It was truth or dare. And both choices were awful. So I was mad. I don't think right when I'm mad. And it's not as if Nancy will ever invite me back."

"Your other friends might, and you'll do it again, just like you always do."

I want to say, Oh, yeah. I forgot about all those other friends. But I don't. "No, I won't. I promise. And I'll let you beat me at Dance Forever."

"I always beat you, anyway. You know, you don't have to hang out with me because you feel sorry for me."

I've never heard that sound in his voice. Bitter. Outside-of-the-lemon-rind bitter. Coffee-without-sugar-and-cream bitter. And I remember how horrible I felt when I learned Mrs. Cruella told the class to be nice to me because of my diabetes. Oh no, you don't, I think. Don't you throw me in the basket with those people.

"Oh My Gatos. I don't feel sorry for you. If I want to hang out with a loser I'll call up Noodlenose. I apologized, didn't I?"

"Well, maybe I don't believe you anymore. Maybe I'm tired of the way you treat people." And with a push-shove, he's gone.

I don't follow, partly because I can't go that fast, and partly because I don't know what else to say. Always keep the door open for a true friend. Well, not if they lock it and throw away the key. I watch River sail around the park. I find a bench and eat a granola bar.

I hate Nancy. This is all her fault. And Sherie's. I hear Danny's voice. Maybe truth or dare can teach us both a lesson. Accept who we are and dare to stand up for ourselves and not trade the truth for other people, no matter what. Before it's too late. Before we lose good friends and disappoint people who love us.

It isn't Nancy's fault. It's my fault. I'm Dinora Diaz. I'm not Flaquita-Danita with the flat tummy. And I'm not Noodlenose Nancy with the fancy house. I have diabetes and love dancing and colors and skateboarding. And I'm River's friend. Maybe, I think. But now he might be my ex-friend.

My phone chirps and I check my text messages.

Group text from Danny to me and River:

Time to go. Meet you in the car.

I look around and see Danny walking to his car that's parked on the street. River skates toward me, then veers away and grinds to a stop. He jumps off his board, ignores me, and heads to Danny's car. I stay a few feet behind him.

"Dinora Diaz?"

I stop and turn. A teenage boy is getting up from a bench at the edge of the park. His foot mushes out his cigarette and he comes over to me.

It's Freddie, from the trailer park. He must have met up with Danny after all. His red ball cap is sideways and he's so tall, taller than Danny, taller than I remember.

"How you been?" He looks at me. Dark eyebrows. Dark eyes. A tattooed teardrop in the corner.

"Good. We moved to an apartment. I miss the trailer park."

"I know. I haven't seen Danny since . . ." He stops, "Since today."

Freddie touches my skateboard. "I see you went pro with that skateboard thing?"

"I'm not very good."

"Nice ride. Show me what you got."

"I can't. I'm leaving." I point to Danny's car.

"Oh, well, next time, then. Hey, Danny says your dad's still gone."

I freeze. Waiting.

"Uncle José says they were together in Mexico, but he doesn't know what happened to your dad. I guess he didn't make it."

I hear Freddie's words but I can't see his face anymore. Everything is black. The sky. The concrete. My head.

"Say hi to your sister and your mom," says Freddie.

I nod like I'm a robot and take a robot step toward Danny's car.

"Hey DeeDee," Freddie calls after me. "Sorry about your dad. Real sorry."

My heart wobbles and falls down into my belly. My skateboard clatters to the ground.

My chest feels broken—my breath is caught in my throat and I can't suck in. I start to run. Freddie calls after me but there's a buzzing in my ears. Like a freight train roaring in my brain. I knew it. Something bad has happened to Papi. He didn't make it. He must be dead. Freddie knows because his Uncle José knows. Everybody knows but me. I pretend I don't hear him and run to the car. I pretend I'm deaf.

I get in the back seat and slam the door.

"What's her problem?" asks Danny.

"I don't know," says River.

I'm deaf. Don't talk to me. What's the sign for that?

"Is it your diabetes? Should we check?" asks Danny.

I'm Deaf DeeDee. Dopey DeeDee. Out my window the sun flashes between the buildings. But I'm in a shadow. Who wants to hear anyway? What good are words?

Danny keeps looking in the rearview mirror.

"Is she sick?" he asks River. "Or hurt?"

"I don't know. I heard her talking to a high-school kid just before we left."

"Maybe she's tired. That was a long day of skating after a sleepover."

They talk as if I'm not here and can't hear. Hear. Here. Yes. Not hearing can make it seem like you're not here.

I feel Danny watching me. Waiting for me to thaw. To be okay. To regain consciousness. But I'm frozen in a deaf coma and I will never be okay.

The car is silent all the way home. What's wrong with me? I don't want to care anymore. About anything. Sleepovers. Skateboarding. Friends. Family. Nobody can make me care. Starting now.

CHAPTER FIFTEEN

D IS FOR DISGRACE

Danny drops us off and goes to work. River walks past me without a word and slams his door. I don't care if he's still mad at me. I don't care about anything anymore. I open the door to our apartment and wish I had my own room for the zillionth time. A room with a door that locked. A room with soundproofing. A room for being alone

Pieces of fabric, paper, envelopes, pictures of dresses, markers are spread all over the couch and chairs and table. Music is blaring. Danita and Andrea are giggling.

"Yay! She's here. DeeDee, look, isn't this the perfect color for everyone? Andrea's grandma is going to make our dresses. I'm going to invite River to be in my court, and he can be your escort. Unless you want to be my *pajes*, but flower girls are usually little. Want to help? We're writing notes to my *quinceañera* court."

I point to the hall and go right back out. As the door closes I hear Andrea. "She must have forgotten something at River's. She'll be back. Don't worry. She'll love it."

I don't know where I'm going. A cocoon place where I can be numb. My skateboard carries me without asking questions and in a few minutes I find myself at Rub-a-Dub-Tub. I go in and find a chair way back in the corner. I put my backpack on the floor. It's not quiet, but it's a silent kind of noisy. The washers hum. The dryers thunk. The kaleidoscope of colors swirl. And I sit in my deaf world. A girl without her Papi.

That's where I am when the washers are mostly empty and the sun sets behind the streaky windows. And that's where I am when Danny sits down across from me.

I look straight into Danny's eyes. "Papi's dead, isn't he?"

"He's not dead."

These are the first words Danny says to me.

My deafness falls away from my ears. "How do you know?"

"Freddie called me. He said you ran away while he was talking to you. Said you looked upset." Danny pulls his phone from his pocket. "I texted you."

I forgot about my phone. I unzip the little front pouch of my backpack and see six text messages from Danny and Danita. None from River. "Freddie said he was real sorry about Papi. He said he didn't make it."

Danny stands up. "Mami is waiting to talk to you."

"I thought you went to work," I say, picking up my skateboard.

"Yes, twice in one week I had to tell my boss my little sister needs rescuing." Danny pats my cheek and picks up my backpack. "After Eddie called me I called Danita and she said River told her he followed you to Rub-A-Dub-Tub. He was worried about you."

I smile. Crazy-detective River. It might not be too late. I want to make it up to both of them. Show Danny how much I love him for being my big brother. Show River I'm sorry about everything and thank him for worrying about me.

Mami and Danita are sitting on the couch when I open the door. Andrea is gone. The TV is off. I don't smell cooking. A bad sign at dinnertime. Mami is holding a tissue and Danita's face is blotchy red from crying.

I want to say something funny. Something to make everything go back to normal. "Why so serious?" I say in Joker's voice, the one from the Batman movie.

"Oh, DeeDee. *Estaba preocupadísima*. I was worried to death." Mami blubbers, then blows her nose in a tissue. But when she lifts her head from the nose blowing she turns on me. A rabid dog. Her voice is hysterical. "*Casco?* Helmet? *No tienes casco?*"

Oh, Land O'Lakes. I didn't think she'd find out I left my helmet at home. Is that why she's crying?

Danny pushes me toward Mami. I smoosh into the space between her and Danita. Danny sits on the arm of the couch.

Mami lets out a whole stream of Spanish in between sobs, and Danita pats her and Danny hands her tissues. She's talking about Papi. I hear two words over and over. *Deportado* and *indocumentado.* I also hear *policía.*

"Did you understand all that?" asks Danny.

I wrinkle my nose. "Not all of it."

"Papi got pulled over for a speeding ticket on his way to work with Freddie's Uncle José in December. But when the police ran his license they found he had been arrested a long time ago before any of us were born, for leaving the scene of an accident, which is a felony."

Mami interrupts. "*No fue su culpa. La culpa era del otro carro, pero se fue.*" Not his fault. There was another car that caused it and left.

Danita sniffles.

"But that was a long time ago. I'm almost eighteen. What's the difference?" says Danny.

"Didn't he pay a fine to get out?" I ask.

Mami looks at Danny. Danny crosses his legs, then uncrosses his legs. "The difference is, Papi is undocumented. No green card. So he received deportation papers all those years ago, but he never left."

Mami wails when he says this. "*Estaba embarazada con Daniel. Y él no quería salir.*" I was pregnant with Daniel and he didn't want to leave.

I don't know what to do. I lean up against her and put my head on her shaking shoulder. My Papi. Undocumented? But he has a wife and three kids and a job.

"Remember how Papi wanted to go to Mexico when Uncle Tito moved back there? Well, that's why," says Danny, running his hands through his hair. "I didn't know."

Danita sniffles again and says, "And before Thanksgiving when he wanted us all to go, I told him he was ruining my life. I told him I hated him."

I think about what I said. All you care about is yourself. When really all he cared about was keeping our family together.

"ICE picked him and Freddie's uncle up the day after he got the ticket. And Mami hasn't heard from him."

"But what about his cell phone? Why didn't he call us? What about *mi bisabuelita* and Uncle Tito? Why don't they call us?"

"He doesn't have his cell phone, or it's not working. I checked to see if he's made any calls from his number."

"What about our relatives? Don't they have cell phones?"

Mami and Danny share a look. It's the DeeDee-is-too-young-to-know look.

"Oh My Gatos. What? I'm old enough to know everything you know about Papi."

Mami speaks rapidly in Spanish and I catch a few words. "*Guerrero*. Very dangerous. Very far away."

Danny says, "Papi is from Tixtla. Close to the capital of Guerrero. Almost two thousand miles from the border. He left when he was a teenager. Met Mami in Jalisco and they immigrated here. Mami doesn't think he has enough money to get back there, and doesn't want to."

"Why?" I ask. If Papi is all alone in Mexico his family should help him.

"The capital of Guerrero, Chilpancingo, has so many murders they close the morgues—you know, where they keep the bodies"

"Where's Uncle Tito? Can't he help Papi?"

"He's in Mexico City. And if Papi doesn't have his phone . . ." Danny trails off.

Poor Papi. Did Mami know this would happen? Why didn't we just go with him? My heart is still beating in my stomach. Thud. Thud. Thud. What's going to happen? How do we know he's okay? It's been so many weeks. "Did you check the trailer park?" I ask. "Maybe he sent us a letter."

"*Sí, sí, pero no sabían a dónde nos mudamos*, they didn't know where we moved." Mami blows her nose. "*Las devolvían*, they returned it."

"Why didn't you tell us?" I ask Mami. "I thought he was dead."

Waves of Spanish words crash from Mami's mouth and I'm not sure I understand.

Danny says, "She didn't want us to think less of Papi. To think he was bad for getting arrested and having a felony and being undocumented. For him to disgrace the family."

Mami looks so sad. "*Lo siento, mijos*. I don't know what to do."

"Well, I wrote to him," I say. "River and I did. We sent emails and letters to every hospital and mission and church in all the border towns."

My whole family stares at me. Like I've grown another head or turned purple with pink polka dots. Then Mami grabs me and squeezes me so hard all that air that was trapped in my throat rushes out.

Danita squeals, "Oh, DeeDee. Oh, DeeDee."

Danny stands up. He rubs his tattooed wrist. "Way to go Gordita."

And silly me, my eyes get wet, and you know how I feel about crying.

•

I don't start waiting for River to text me until Sunday afternoon. I know he's got church and sometimes family get-togethers. I go out to the parking lot and check for his mom's car over and over. But it's not there. Where did he go? He didn't tell me he was going anywhere.

After dinner Danny takes Danita to a basketball tournament at the high school. Mami goes to bed. I stay up and wait for them to come home. I still hope for a text message from River. But nothing. I think about texting him to tell him the news about Papi. But I don't.

When my text alert goes off, I jump. It's a number I don't recognize.

> **This is River. I think I left my phone in Danny's car. Ask him if I can check.**
>
> Me: **He's not home. I'll bring it to you when he gets back.**
>
> River: **No. I'll get it myself.**
>
> Me: **If it's late and I find it I'll bring it to school. Where have you been?**

I wait for him to text back, but he doesn't. He must be using his mom's phone.

I get ready for couch and I'm drifting off to skateboard dancing heaven when the click of the lock startles me. Danny tiptoes in and hangs his keys on the hook.

Danita whispers, "She's so cute when she's sleeping, isn't she?"

Danny mumbles something about high maintenance not being cute.

Danita whispers back, "Yah. Cute as a pain in the butt."

I grit my teeth and pretend to be asleep. It's not Papi who's a disgrace. It's me.

I don't want to bother Danny for River's phone, so once I hear him finish brushing his teeth and close his bedroom door, I grab his keys and do my own tiptoeing out and down the hall to the stairs. It's spooky being in the parking lot in the dark and I hope nobody sees me in my princess pj's. When I get to Danny's car I dig around in the front seat and sure enough, I find River's phone jammed in between the seat cushions. It's after ten-thirty. Too late to call or knock. First thing in the morning I'll bring it to him.

But when I get back to my couch a voice in my ear says, "Yoo hoo. You there. Don't you want to sneak a peek at his phone? You know his pass code. Now's your chance. I won't tell." Actually disgrace should be my middle name.

And I know it's a rotten thing to do. Creeping around on his phone. Don't judge. First I look at his photos. They're mostly selfies of us. Skating. Drawing. At the library. And a few of him and Yari at SLT and him and Colin.

Then I see a new app called Padlet. It sounds like a farm game or maybe something like Minecraft. When I open it there's a list of dates, and each date opens a new bulletin board. Each bulletin board has a jumble of poems,

diary entries, photos, graphics, emoticons. I pull up the
first one and scan over it. A little text box has the words:

> *I met a girl today*
> *On the balcony.*
> *A colorful girl.*
> *One who hears.*
> *Will she want*
> *To be friends with me?*

There's a scan of the drawing he gave me in the
hospital. And a link to an article about diabetes. I don't
know what to think. It's cool, but it's weird.

I hit another date, this time in February.

It's a journal page.

> *All I want in the world is to be a normal boy. But if*
> *I can't be a normal boy, then I want to be a good friend.*
> *I'm scared about going to Robert Frost tomorrow. I'm*
> *scared I won't be able to do things like the hearing kids.*
> *I'm scared I might get hurt without adaptive equipment.*
> *And I'm scared the teachers might be frustrated teaching*
> *me. But at least I have one friend already. I know she will*
> *help me make a good start. She's so creative and funny.*
> *I like that she says what's on her mind and wants to try*
> *new things. I'm so lucky DeeDee moved next door.*

I have to close my eyes after I read that one. And squeeze them tight. I was a horrible friend. I made everything even worse for River. But he was still a good friend to me. What a disgrace I am.

Another date in February.

> *I don't forgive people because I'm weak.*
> *I forgive them because I'm strong enough*
> *To understand people make mistakes.*

A drawing of the jungle gym. A girl sits at the top. Me. A girl stands at the bottom with her leg out. Nancy. And two boys hold a soccer ball together. River and Colin.

Then I open a date from a week ago. In the text box it says:

> *I found out DeeDee made fun of me with her friends.*
> *I never should have trusted her in the first place.*
> *She's as shallow as a kiddie pool.*
> *Forgiving someone is easy, but being able to trust*
> *them again is a whole different story.*

There's a few photos of the latest skateboard shoe advertisements with his speech bubbles added—*saving my money*, and *can't wait until my birthday*. There's also a really cool drawing of a kid on a shark-shaped skateboard doing a vertical on a cloud. The shark has a piece of the cloud in its teeth. I can't believe how good River's art is.

I go to the first date in March. A drawing of the Starship Enterprise, the *Star Trek* ship. Under the drawing River wrote:

> *" Resistance is futile."*

And under that he wrote:

> *I will not let my distinctions make me feel weak or afraid. I will not let others force me to be someone I'm not. I will accept myself. I'm doing the best I can.*

I open the last entry.

> *Today's the saddest day.*
> *I told myself everyone makes mistakes.*
> *I told myself at least I had one friend,*
> *Even if it was only for half the time.*
> *But my mom always says*
> *People don't deserve second and third chances*
> *Until they learn from their mistakes.*
> *So after today I will be one friend less.*

What is wrong with me? I don't deserve any chances. I'm a disgrace to the human race. I shut down Padlet.

I almost shut down his phone, but it's as if I have no control over my fingers.

I scroll through his text messages until I see one from Yari.

Yari: **Do you know DD?**

River: **Yes. Why?**

Yari: **Did you see her freak out in the lunchroom?**

River: **No, but she's my friend.**

Yari: **Oh, sorry. I get tired of all that drama, don't you?**

River: **I guess sometimes.**

I turn off the phone. I want to throw it out the window. I can't believe Yari bad-mouthed me to River. At first I'm boiling mad, then after a few seconds it comes to me that River never really said anything bad about me back to Yari. He could have. There's plenty of bad to say.

I put my face to the back of the couch and let big drops of water come out of my eyes for all my lost pepitas. No seeds of friendship. No seeds of hope. No seeds for seeds.

I started this. It's all my fault. Everybody hates me.

CHAPTER SIXTEEN

D IS FOR DECISION

I wake up with a headache, and it gets worse when River's phone alarm buzzes on the coffee table. I throw the phone in my backpack for safekeeping. Sometime in the middle of the night I made a decision. I want to plant my seeds again. I'm done with lying seeds and stealing seeds. And I'm done with two-face disgrace seeds.

I lift up the couch cushion and push my hand way down the back where there's a little fabric sling. I pull out all the things I've stolen. It takes four fistfuls to get it all. I stuff them all in my backpack. Done.

I know you're thinking about that hoodie, aren't you? The one I stole on my first day? Well, I'll have you know I already left that in the hall. It didn't even fit me.

Mami rushes in with my insulin. "Gordita, *se me olvido. No me levante en la noche.*"

She forgot to test me in the night? That explains the headache.

By the time I take care of everything and eat breakfast I know I've missed the opportunity to stop by River's. I will just have to give him his phone at school.

Yari is her usual cheery self in peer tutoring. Blabbing about her weekend and River's Lucky Shamrock Fundraiser idea. When she goes to print my report I put her pom-pom back.

"Are you ready for tryouts?" Mrs. Marsh asks when she tests me.

"I think I'm going to dance," I say.

"Oh, well, that will be a challenge." She sounds disappointed that I'm not skating. "But no matter what, I'm so proud of you. One of my special students. Trying out."

I see River's backpack but not River when I get to room #13_. Mrs. Cruella collects everyone's phones at the beginning of the day, but River might get mad if I turn his in for him. I switch it to silent and bury it deep down in an outside pocket he never uses. When he gets to class I'll tell him I put it there. I leave the little coin purse on the shelf where I found it. And I put the pencils and erasers in the pencil cup. There's not much I can do about the bags of chips and cookies I took from the lunch basket. But those I will pay forward. Like a movie I once watched.

When River walks in with his homework, he goes right to Mrs. Cruella and hands her his phone. He sits down and I hear him whisper to Colin, "Must be going crazy. My phone was in my backpack the whole time."

•

"How's your boyfriend?"

You'll never guess who sat down across from me at lunch. I'm going to pretend I can't even hear her. The sleepover comes rushing back to me. How Noodlenose called my family illegal. If she ever finds out Papi got deported, the whole school will know she was right.

"You're lucky my mom isn't going to call her lawyer," Noodlenose says. Then she announces to the table, "DeeDee almost broke my phone and ripped my bathrobe."

"Should we invite your boyfriend to eat with us?" She makes chopstick motions with her fingers.

I wish I could move to another table—or even better, back to Lincoln Elementary. I shove the rest of my lunch in my mouth and head to the bathroom. River is talking to some fifth graders at the next table, leaning way over so he can hear them in the loud lunchroom, and they're all laughing.

I have the same kind of ripping feeling in my heart as when Danny went to NGYCP and Papi went away. Not the same, exactly, much smaller, but still the same sad and lonely rip. And something else. Kind of a burning. Not exactly jealous. But a wish that never comes true. A longing.

Samantha and Nicole come stand in line next to me.

Nicole points at the poster. "So you're trying out."

"Tryouts are really stressful," says Samantha.

"Why aren't you?" I ask them.

"I'd never make it. It's really competitive," says Nicole.

"They choose the best from every grade," says Samantha. "Nancy was in it last year."

Of course she was. She probably started dancing when she was a baby. She probably came out dancing. She probably doesn't even need dance lessons.

"You'll do fine, DeeDee. You're a good dancer," says Nicole.

After it's too late, I think about all the things I could have said to Nicole and Samantha. Why don't you play your flute, Samantha? I hear you in the band sometimes when I go to Mrs. Marsh. And you're a good dancer, too, Nicole. Just as good as me. We should practice together. Oh, what's the point of trying have a friend, be a friend when I can't even say the right things?

•

The week marches along. No texts from River. No after school fun. I've got yards and yards of time on my hands. I clean up the house for Mami, put away my sheet and blanket everyday—in case Danny wants to bring a friend home. I do my homework and even some extra-credit work. I read my book and watch *American Idol*. I think about inviting Nicole or Samantha over after school, but why bother. They'll have some excuse.

Danita and Andrea let me help put together some of the decorations for the *quinceañera*. Danita brings a piece of cerulean-blue fabric over to the table where we're making flowers. It's the material she tried to show me the day I thought Papi was dead.

"Do you like it, DeeDee? We picked it especially for you. You will look so pretty dancing in this."

It's the same blue from Nancy's bathroom, but with glittery sparkles, tinier than sequins, and it's soft and silky. I love it. I really love it. And I will love dancing in it, even Mexican dances. "It's nice," I tell Danita. "But not strapless."

"Like you could hold up a strapless dress, silly," Danita scoffs.

"Whatever."

"Where's River? If he's going to be your escort he needs to practice," says Danita.

"He's busy," I say.

"If he's not here tomorrow, we'll practice without him," she says.

Then I think of something that never crossed my mind before. "Who's your escort?"

Andrea makes a slicing motion across her throat.

"None of your business," says Danita to me, and she huffs off to the bedroom to put away the material.

"Boy trouble," whispers Andrea.

So, even drop-dead-gorgeous-skinny-as-a-taquito girls have problems? That's at least encouraging, isn't it?

•

The SLT's shamrocks for St. Patrick's Day are selling like hot tamales. I bought one for Mrs. Marsh. I wrote, *You're lucky I don't come see you more often.* She went bananas over it and hung it on her door. Most everybody in room #13_ has received a lucky shamrock, and some people have received more than one. And at least one person we both know has received none. I bought three more shamrocks for a little project I'm starting at home because have a friend be a friend isn't limited to Robert Frost, is it?

When I get home from school, we all practice dancing the *quinceañera* songs—me, Danita and Andrea.

When Danny comes in after work, he dances *"El Vals De La Mariposa"* with Danita so he'll be ready in case Papi isn't here. Then he dances *"El Jarabe Tapatío"* with me. It's my favorite.

"I wish I could have a *quinceañera* for my fifteenth birthday," says Andrea. "All I'm getting is a new bedroom set."

"Won't you have a sweet sixteen birthday?" asks Danita. "I thought that's the tradition in the United States."

"Maybe. As long as it doesn't cost too much," says Andrea.

When Mami comes home, she claps and cries watching us, which is embarrassing. I tell everyone that I've decided to dance *"El Jarabe Tapatío"* for the Spring Fling. Mami claps some more and wipes her eyes. Danny says if I make it he won't miss it. Danita asks Mami if she can skip school to watch me and Mami says no. Andrea whispers that her mom might let her skip.

While Mami makes dinner I get to work on my project. River told me that Mrs. Robinson's husband died last year. That's why she seems so crabby all the time. Not just because she has a giant coffee monster in front of her door. I decide a few jokes might make her smile. I have to be careful not to write any jokes about husbands or death. I write the jokes on the back of the shamrocks and draw little cartoons.

•

Thursday and Friday I try to concentrate on my unfinished school assignments. Mrs. Cruella gives us a second chance to turn in unfinished work to erase a zero before she puts the grades on our report cards. River, Samantha, Colin and Hannah are caught up with everything so get to choose extra art or computer. The four of them happily buzz away, abandoning us worker bees and our incompleted tasks River comes back for his blue ball that he needs for art. He walks right by me without a glance. I get it. I don't blame him. He gave me so many chances.

At lunch I slide down the bench to the very end, by the wall, so Nancy can't bother me. I hear Sherie's loud voice. "Who wants to meet at the mall tomorrow?"

"I can't," says Nancy. "I have dance at ten."

"Are you practicing for the tryouts at dance?" asks Nicole.

"I'm actually practicing for a competition in New York," says Nancy. "I wish our Spring Fling was limited to only dancing. It'd be so much better."

"What's wrong with singing?" asks Hannah. "I like singing."

"Then you should try out," says Nancy.

"I'm not that good," says Hannah. "I heard somebody is skateboarding this year."

"Skateboarding? That's not a talent. That's a joke on wheels," says Nancy. They laugh.

I chew and chew so my mouth stays busy. I'd like to see Nancy try skateboarding. More than that, I'd like to see her fall flat on her you-know-what. Even better, I'd like the SLT to choose me instead of her for the Spring Fling. Wouldn't that make a dent in her you-know-what?

•

Danita's in her room when I get home. "Hey, want to go to the mall tomorrow?" I call to her

She opens her door and peeks out. Little streaks of eyeliner puddle at the corner of her eyes. "Not really," she says. "Go eat a snack." Then she goes back into her room and closes the door. Hmm. Must still be having boy troubles.

I practice "*El Jarabe Tapatío*" until I've memorized all the steps. Then I practice it again with my eyes closed.

Danita rushes out of her room and opens the front door before Andrea even knocks. Andrea gives me a thumbs-up and they disappear. Maybe the boy troubles are on the mend.

I finish decorating the shamrocks and put the first one under Mrs. Robinson's door. Then I do my homework and dance one more time. Danny comes home and stretches out on the couch.

"How was work?" I ask.

"So many boxes to stock. Stuff for Easter baskets. Stuff for St. Patrick's Day. I'm so tired," he says.

Mami comes zipping through the door carrying a huge, flat box. "Danita, *ven aca*, come here. *Mira*, Gordita. *Mira*. From my friend Rosalinda for your trying out."

She puts the box on the coffee table and when she opens it a dress bursts right out of the box. It's an explosion of color, like a peacock's plumes, but instead of blues and greens, it's mango-tango orange. The layers remind me of upside-down cupcake liners, overlapping, edged with rainbows.

"Wow," says Andrea.

"I can't wear that," I tell Mami.

She pulls it over my head and ties the sash into a big bow in the back. "Take off jeans," she says.

I rustle to the bathroom and pull off my jeans from under the dress. When I turn to go out I see myself in the mirror. My long dark hair. My suntanned face. My mango-tango dress. I look so Mexican. Like a Mexican folk dancer. I don't know if I love it or hate it.

When I come out, everyone claps. "Try dancing in it," says Danita. "What song?"

"*El Jarabe Tapatio*," I say.

The music starts and poor tired Danny takes my hand. He spins me and the dress swirls around me like a triple-decker merry-go-round. Halfway through the song

Danny passes me to Danita, blowing me a kiss on his way to night school. Mami has her hands pressed to her heart.

"*Esto es increíble, bella como una flor,*" says Mami.

"OMG DeeDee. Mami's right. It's incredible. Like a flower," says Danita.

"Just like the *folklorico* dancers," says Andrea.

Mami kisses me and tells me to take good care of the borrowed dress. I go change.

I hear Andrea and Danita talking to Mami.

"I got a new bedroom set, so we don't need my bunk bed anymore," says Andrea.

"It will make sleepovers so much easier, Mami," says Danita. "Please let me have it."

"How much?" asks Mami.

"Can it be a present for your *quinceañera?*" asks Andrea.

Danita squeals. "Oh, Andrea. You're the best."

That little burning feeling works its way up from my stomach to my heart and then to my throat. It burns enough that my eyes get a little watery. Nope. I tell myself. I'm not going to be jealous of Danita. I'm going to be glad she has a best friend. Danita deserves a best friend. Of course a best friend doesn't equal Papi, but it helps.

I come out of the bathroom and Danita is jumping up and down. "DeeDee. Andrea is giving me her bunk bed. How would you like to share a room with your bossy sister?"

The burning in my throat bursts into giggly bubbles. "I don't have a bossy sister," I say. "I have the best
sister in the world."

"We paint. You choose color," says Mami and goes
to start dinner.

"What color paint?" asks Andrea.

"What about light gray?" says Danita.

"Gray? That's not even a color. It's the absence of
color. What about Wisteria or Purple Mountains' Maj-
esty?" I say.

"OMG, DeeDee. We're not picking out nail polish.
It's a bedroom, *tontita*."

CHAPTER SEVENTEEN

D IS FOR DISAPPOINTMENT

Why is it that when you can't wait for something to happen, time goes so slow? But when you dread something coming, it sneaks up lickety-split? Before I blink, it's the end of the weekend and the day before the tryout. And all of a sudden, I'm not sure I want to try out, even though I've practiced "*El Jarabe Tapatio*" one million times, at least. Everyone in my family thinks I'm really good. And everyone thinks I'm really going to try out. Everyone but me. I don't know what I'm going to do.

They are all so excited. I'm all so nervous.

Mami hums and twirls. "Your Papi would be so proud."

Andrea and Danita did my hair last night and made me sleep in a scarf. Danny is driving me to school with the dress in a garment bag that Andrea borrowed from her friend. I take the dress to Mrs. Marsh first thing and she hangs it in her closet. I try to think of ways to escape trying out. During language arts I think, pretend to be sick. During math I think, get in trouble at lunch. During reading group I think, run away to Mexico. It's the longest day in the world.

During art, I watch Noodlenose walk by and take something off River's table while he's at the sink rinsing out his paintbrush. Then I see River searching all around and on the floor. He leans over and says something to his seat neighbor, Colin, and they both start looking.

I inch forward a bit so Noodlenose is in my sight-line. She's busy working on her painting, but peeking out from under her elbow is something blue—River's blue hand aid ball.

I'm thinking about what to do. This is my chance to show him I do learn from my mistakes. That I deserve another chance. But what should I do? Tell River? Tell Mr. Leverance? Or go take the ball and put it on River's table? He hates being embarrassed by a big scene. But Nancy shouldn't be allowed to get away with it. I can't decide what River would like better. But while I'm chewing it around in my mind, Colin walks right up to Noodlenose's table and holds out his hand.

"What?" I hear her say.

"Want me to tell?" Colin says.

Noodlenose makes a sour-pickle face and slams the ball into Colin's hand. Colin puts the ball on River's table and they high five, or as River says, high three. When River sees me watching, he signs something to Miss Monaldo. I recognize one word: DeeDee. It's easy because it's two times the sign for D. She signs back. My name again. They both stare at me.

I'm sure River is tattling on me not lifting a finger to help get his ball. Now Miss Monaldo knows what a bad friend I am. And what a disappointment. I'm so done with Robert Frost Elementary. I hope we move again. I hope we all move to Mexico. I need a do-over, or like Mami says, a start-over. I'm sick of this awful rocky lump in my stomach. Next time I'll start out on the right foot.

When the bell rings, I get the dress and head out the little kid door. No one will see me ditching the tryouts. Probably no one will even care. I'll get home before Danny comes to pick me up from the tryouts. I'm standing on the edge of the street, waiting for the crossing guard. The line of cars stretches out the parking lot and into the street. I'll never be able to cross. I've just decided to walk through the building to the cross-walk on the other side when Principal Sorry touches my arm.

"DeeDee? Mrs. Marsh tells me you're trying out for our Spring Fling."

"Uh—yah, I was," I stammer.

"I see your mother dropped off your costume. Well, good luck, I hope you make it. Here, let me help you." And to my horror, she takes the garment bag and starts walking back to the door.

"Hey, I—" but I don't finish because about a million little kindergarteners run down the sidewalk screaming. They cut right in front of me and before I know it, Principal Sorry walks back into the school.

By the time I get to the auditorium, a line of kids snakes down the hall and around the corner. Some I know. Noodlenose, for one. Most I don't. Kids of all sizes. Fluting. Trumpeting. Banging. Twirling. Even cartwheeling and cheering. But where is Principal Sorry with my dress?

Maybe I should call Danny to get me. Now. And get my dress tomorrow. And, I realize, be a disappointment to my family and Mrs. Marsh and all the kids with diabetes and Principal Sorry and River and probably everybody on the planet. But this line will take hours and hours and I can't wait. Danny will be late for night school and that's not even a made-up excuse. Besides that, I forgot to get a snack when I was in the nurse's office, so I might even pass out. And that's not even a made-up excuse, either.

A teacher pops her head out of the tryout room door. "Quiet down out here." She looks down the hall and motions to me. "Stand in line until you're called."

I slide to the end of the line.

"No playing instruments in the hall. We are taking auditions in the order of sign-ups." The teacher closes the door.

"What are you doing for the tryouts?" asks the little girl in front of me.

"Dancing," I say.

"We're dancing, too. We're best friends. We have matching outfits." Her friend smiles at me and they hold hands.

"Where are you going to change?" I ask, wondering where their outfits are.

"We don't have to wear our outfits for the tryout. Only if we make it."

I look down the line. Not one person is wearing a dance outfit or costume. Why didn't someone tell me this? Why didn't Mrs. Marsh tell me when I brought my dress in her office? Why didn't Principal Sorry tell me when she took my dress from me? Why didn't my best friend tell me the rules? Oh, yah, I don't have a best friend, do I? I watch the two little girls giggle and whisper and I feel sorry for myself.

I decide to stand here in line until I figure out what to do. Call Danny and then go get the dress. Or get the dress and walk home. Or get the dress tomorrow and face Mami's explosion today.

"Dinora Diaz," yells a voice. "Dinora Diaz."

I jolt from my thoughts and troop to the tryout door.

"Hope you make it," say the best friends at the same time.

"Break a leg, Dinora Dinosaura," says Noodlenose when I walk past her. "Hope you don't crash through the stage."

"Hope I do," I say over my shoulder. "Then you'll fall all the way to France where they'll see your underpants." I hear kids laughing but I don't turn around.

I open the door and Mrs. Marsh, Mrs. Cruella, and Principal Sorry wave at me from the other side of the auditorium. Danny stands near the exit door at the back. Yari and River and some fifth graders I don't know are sitting in the front row. Oh My Gatos. Now I really don't know what to do.

Danny gives me a thumbs-up.

"DeeDee, eat this before you go backstage and change," says Mrs. Marsh, rushing over and handing me a granola bar.

"I don't think—" I start to say.

Principal Sorry holds out the dress. "You don't have to put it on, but I'd love to see this dress."

Mr. Leverance comes rushing into the room. "Did I miss it? Oh, no I didn't. Oh, that dress! *Viva México!*" He claps his hand over his heart.

Good Gatos. I give myself a pep talk while I zip behind the curtain, rip open the granola bar, and slip the dress over my head. You've got nothing to lose. You won't make it, anyway. You may as well just put the ridiculous dress on and dance and be done with it. Make people happy. I struggle with the bow in the back. I know it looks hideous. Where's Mami when I need her?

I can do this with effort and work. My growth mindset. I stand in the center of the stage. The curtain opens. I see Yari and River whispering and giggling. I'm one millisecond from walking out but the music starts. "*El Jarabe Tapatio.*" I shut off my brain and let the music wash over me. Let it become the master of my legs and my arms. I'm a spinning top, a twirling merry-go-round, floating and free. I reach for the sky and fall to the earth, the wings of my dress making rotating pinwheels of fireworks all around the stage.

I take a quick peek at the SLT members. River shakes his head and says something to Yari, who starts writing in her notebook. I must look ridiculous in this dress dancing to this music. He hates it. They all hate it. I hide my hands in the folds of the dress and make the twirls smaller.

The SLT stops the music after three minutes. That's the rule of the tryout. Three minutes. If you make it for the Spring Fling, then you can have five minutes. I finish swirling, people clap, and the curtains close. I run down the steps into the auditorium. My face is on fire. I can't believe I made a fool of myself in front of all these people.

"Good job, DeeDee," says Yari.

River's eyes are big like he wants to say something to me, but his lips are straight and pinched shut like they won't let his mouth speak.

"I stunk like a skunk," I say to the entire world. I'm nothing but a disappointment. Forget about growth mindset. This is too hard.

I grab the garment bag and my backpack and go out the back door with Danny. "Don't say anything," I say to Danny on the drive home. "I told you I wasn't good enough."

Danny drops me in front of our apartment. "Stop being so hard on yourself. You did fine," he says. "Tell Mami I'm meeting with my mentor tonight to find out about the spring training program."

The spring training program? Another disappointing thing. How will I survive without Danny here for six weeks?

Mami is snoozing on the couch when I open the apartment door. My plate of cold chicken and rice waits for me on the table. Talk about a disappointment. It's quiet. Danita must be at Andrea's. I watch Mami's boring show, afraid to change the channel and disturb her.

When Mami wakes up, she asks me about the try-outs, hangs the mango-tango dress in the front closet, and then goes to bed early. I turn off the TV, test my blood sugar and give myself a shot. I make my couch bed and feel sorry for myself.

One time I asked River, "Did you miss your dad when he died?"

He said he was too little to remember his dad, but that it was like losing a tooth. When it's in your mouth you don't think about it, but when it's gone, you notice the hole all the time.

And that's exactly the way I feel tonight. All those days when Papi came home from work and everything was normal, I never told him, I'm so glad you're home or I'm sure glad I have a daddy who loves me. But now there's a hole, a space. No Papi to kiss me good night or call me Gordita or kick the soccer ball. No Papi to escort Danita or dance the "*Vals de la Mariposa*" at her *quinceañera*. No Papi to give the toast, or twirl me around.

I snuggle under my haunted madrina blanket with my teddy and start to read my school library book about a dog and a girl who's missing her mother just like I'm missing my father, and I get all entwined in my dreams with the dog at Danita's *quinceañera* and a boy skateboarding between giant orange flowers that twirl like a mango-tango dress.

I jerk awake. My phone is ringing. River's calling me. I know it. I stumble over to my backpack and fumble in the pouch to grab it. Oh, don't let him hang up.

"Make it so," I demand into the phone. But it's not River's number. It's nobody's number. It says UNKNOWN CALLER. I hear static and I'm about to hang up.

But then a deep voice says, "*Mi Lora Hermosa.*"

The flutter of a thousand wings beats against the walls of my heart. "Papi? Papi? Is it really you?" My stomach flips and flops and flips and flops.

"Gordita, your letter. Your letter came to me at *Casa del Immigrante. Te quiero, mi gordita.* You've saved my life," he says, his voice breaking. "My phone stolen. All my numbers gone. My letters returned. My hope all gone."

"The trailer park burned down, Papi. We moved. I sent you our new address," I say. There's so much to tell him.

"*Ay, Dios mío.* Is everybody good? I missed your birthday."

Too many words ping-pong off the walls in my head. "It's okay. We're all good. Danita's planning for her *quinceañera.* Danny's home and he's going to do the first dance with her. And Mami works two jobs."

"Daniel? *Mi hijo?*"

"He's good Papi. He's got his GED. He might be recommended for a military placement for training." My heart expands in my chest when I say this. I'm so proud of Danny. Did I ever tell him? I have to tell him.

"Tell him I've missed him. And how proud I am. And you, *mija querida?*" Papi asks.

I want to tell Papi about disappointing everyone at the tryouts. About having diabetes. About skateboarding and about River. About Nancy and Sherie. But there's too much to tell. What's the most important thing?

"Papi, I have a friend, but he's mad at me. And it's my fault. I've been a bad friend and I don't know what to do." I sniffle. I know I have to wake up Mami, but I want one more minute with my Papi.

"DeeDee. Get a paper and write this down," Papi says.

I pull my reading response journal from my backpack. "Okay, Papi."

"This is a poster here. Write the word 'friends.' Now this is what friends do. F—fight for you. R—respect you. I—include you. E—encourage you. N—need you. D—deserve you. S—stand by you." Papi waits for me to copy everything down. Then he says, "This is good, no? This is what you do for your friend."

"*Sí,* Papi. *Sí.*" I look at what I wrote. Yes. I can do all these things. Even if River never speaks to me again. "Papi, are you coming home?"

"I don't know, *mija*. I don't know. Maybe you will visit me here until there's a way."

"*Te echamos de menos*, Papi." I've waited to say this for so long. I'm not even sure the Spanish is right. We miss you.

Papi laughs. "Your Spanish, Gordita. *Ay, Dios mio.* Worse than my English. You will laugh at my job here. I'm the English translator for the *immigrantes* who arrive that don't speak English."

I laugh. "You're mixed up, Papi. English in Mexico and Spanish in the United States."

"Remember *mija, amistades verdaderas, mantienen las puertas abiertas.* Remember my *Star Trek*? Go boldly . . ." he waits for me to finish.

"Where no man has gone before," I say. River would really like my papi. "I have to go get Mami," I say.

"*Te quiero*, DeeDee," he says.

"*Te quiero*, Papi," I say.

"Mami! Danny, Danita!" I yell at the top of my lungs.

Mami rushes out, one arm halfway in a bathrobe sleeve, the other arm backstroking to grab the other one. "*Mija*, are you sick?"

Danny stands in his doorway. Blinking and worried.

I hold my phone above my head and shout like a warrior, like a champion, like a lottery winner, "It's Papi!"

Mami snatches the phone from me. Danny hovers close by. I hug them both. But then Mami gets blubbery and you know how I feel about crying. It's a good time to go to the bathroom. I smile into the mirror. I pump my fists into the air. I look ridiculous and that's okay. Because Papi's okay. Oh My Gatos. Where's Danita? Still sleeping?

I rush into her bedroom and shake her awake. "Danita, Papi's on the phone."

She rolls over. "Go away, DeeDee."

"No, Danita. Wake up. It's Papi." I jiggle her mattress.

"That's not funny, DeeDee." She pulls her pillow over her head.

I yank her pillow. I switch on her bedside light. I scream in her face, "It's Papi!"

She stares at me. Squints. Suspicious. I smile my ridiculous smile. She blinks. Her eyebrows lift. Her eyes widen. She catapults from her bed and pushes me out of the way. "Papi!" she wails. I sit on the edge of Danita's bed and squeeze my arms around my stomach to make it stop jumping.

CHAPTER EIGHTEEN

D IS FOR DANCE

Stop asking me. Stop, I want to scream at Mami. Because they haven't posted the list for Spring Fling yet.

Do not tell me one more time I was great. Do not, I want to scream at Danny. Because he doesn't know how great everybody else probably was.

You'll be the first to know. The first, I want to scream at Mrs. Marsh. Because she will see the list in the office before they post it.

I have so many other things on my mind. Papi in a shelter. Danny going away. Danita's *quinceañera*. And

River, still not speaking to me. Knowing Papi is safe lifted the giant storm over my head, but a shadowy cloud still floats in front of my sunny day. I miss River. I think about his Padlet poems and his text messages. I think about him whispering and giggling during my tryout. I think about him signing about me to Miss Monaldo.

Thursday is Mami's day off, so she and Danny finish the bedroom. They paint three walls gray and one wall pink. We set up the bunk beds and put our new bedspreads on.

Mami says, "*Perfecto*."

I smell dinner—rice boiling for *agua de horchata*, pork roasting for *torta de avocados*, and chicken bubbling for *pozole*. Mami's been so happy since Papi called. Humming and singing and joking and laughing. It makes us forget Danny is leaving in two weeks.

I wake up to rain tapping on the window, close to my head where I'm sleeping in the top bunk. Danita got first choice of the bottom bunk. She gives me a squinty-eye crabby look. "What?" I ask. "I didn't mean to step on your head in the night. Mami has to test me." When I get to school I'm wet from walking in the rain and late for my Friday morning tutoring. Yari left a message with the door monitor that she went to sell shamrocks.

Those darn shamrocks. But wait. Lucky shamrocks. I dig around in my jacket pocket and find a quarter. I reach my fingers into the little cracks in the pouches of my backpack and find two dimes and a nickel and head to the library and buy one shamrock from an SLT member I don't know.

Then I stop into Mrs. Marsh's office, and while I wait for her, I decorate the shamrock with little skateboards and *Star Trek* logos. In the middle I write. *I'm lucky I have a friend like you and not like me.* I slide it into my back pocket.

Mrs. Marsh bustles in and tests me. We both look out in the hall when we hear an uproar near the office door.

"They must have posted the Spring Fling list," says Mrs. Marsh.

"Go see, DeeDee," says Mrs. Marsh, showing me her crossed fingers.

I'm sure my name isn't on the list, but I'm curious about whose is.

That's when I hear Noodlenose's needle-sharp voice say, "Who wants to watch Bubblebutt dance, anyway?"

I freeze.

Then I hear River's voice. "Don't be jealous just because you didn't make it."

"They just picked her because they felt sorry for her, a Mexican with diabetes, probably illegal."

"You don't know that," says River.

"Ha. Yes I do. I heard Mr. Leverance tell Mrs. Krewell that after all DeeDee's been through this year Spring Fling should be handed to her on a platter."

"You know what?" I hear River say. "I feel sorry for you. It must be hard work to be so mean." Then, "Hey! That's my backpack."

I watch Noodlenose run and River chase her, and I escape back to Mrs. Marsh's office.

"Congratulations, DeeDee. I knew you'd make it."

My hands are shaking. I start to inject myself without using the alcohol wipes first.

"DeeDee. You forgot to swab."

I start over. Bubblebutt. Bubblebutt. I can't stop Noodlenose's voice in my head. Don't be jealous. Don't be jealous. I can't stop River's voice. I feel sorry for you. I even hear Mr. Leverance. On a platter. On a platter. I poke myself and see red. On my thigh and in my head. Red for blood and anger.

Now I know what River means. People being nice because they feel sorry for you. Because you have a defect that makes you not as perfect as they are. So they do you a huge favor. Show you what a great person they are. Give you a break that, if you were normal, you wouldn't deserve. Because you are inferior.

I march right out of Mrs. Marsh's office without even saying goodbye. I'm a big bundle of mad.

First—I'm a good dancer. I know this. I always get the highest score on the Dance Forever game.

Second—if they voted for me just because I have diabetes, then I better show them that, diabetes or not,

I'm a better dancer than any fourth grader they've ever seen.

And third—if they voted for me just because I'm Mexican then why didn't they vote for Nancy just because she's Asian? And she doesn't know anything about my family. This is where we live. This is our country. That's all she needs to know.

In my head I know Nancy is wrong and River's right. She's jealous because I'm going to dance in front of the whole school.

Oh My Gatos. I'm going to dance in front of the whole school. My knees wobble when I think about it.

The tardy bell rings. Mrs. Krewell—that's how you really say my teacher's name—knows I'm always late, so I don't worry. And I was wrong about her anyway. She's a good teacher. I should never have called her Cruella.

I want to put the shamrock in River's backpack, but I don't see it hanging in the hall. And he's not in the classroom, either. Maybe he had an SLT meeting, I think. But when he doesn't show up after fifteen minutes I know something's wrong.

"I forgot something at the nurse," I tell Mrs. Krewell. I fly into the boy's bathroom and look under the stall doors. I don't see any feet, for sure not River's blue Nike SB Dunks. I walk-run to the library. Maybe he's helping put away shamrock stuff, or counting the fundraising money. I heard they made enough to rent an outside stage for Spring Fling. But no River.

I flat-out run to the art room. But there's only Mr. Leverance moving some paintings to a drying rack. Did he really say hand it to her on a platter? You know, I bet he didn't. I bet Noodlenose got it wrong.

Where else could River be? Think like a detective, I tell myself. What's the meanest thing Nancy would do with River's backpack?

And just like that, I know. I'm out on the wet playground in two seconds. And there's River. On the third level of the jungle gym. And there's his backpack. Balanced between two rungs. Way at the top. On the fifth level. And if River tries to go any higher, he'll never be able to climb down. Even his blue hand-aid ball doesn't help on slippery jungle gym.

"Hey, stop," I yell, waving my arms wildly to get his attention. He turns and circles both arms around a metal pipe. His pale face stares down at me. His eyes perfect circles. His mouth sucking in breaths.

In a second I've scrambled up to his level, and I sit, swinging my legs over the bar. He carefully lowers himself down next to me. It's not raining anymore, but the bars are slick.

"You don't have to help me," he says, his voice shaking.

"I know." I nod and look right into his eyes.

"I can do this," he says, his knuckles whitening.

"I know."

We sit there, quiet, for a while, like two birds. Wishing we could fly away to a better world.

"You didn't have to stand up for me," I tell him, my voice ashamed.

"I know."

"Are you nice because you feel sorry for me?" I ask.

"No." He says it so loud he almost loses his grip. "Are you?"

"No, I don't feel sorry for you, either. You helped me look for my dad, right? You taught me about skateboarding, right? You practiced dancing with me, right?"

"Yah, but . . ."

"So, did you do those things because you felt sorry for me?"

"Of course not. I'm good at those things, so I did them."

"Right. And I'm good at climbing this jungle gym. Better than you." I carefully pull myself up and anchor my feet on the bar. I stretch my hands to the next level and the next level, and my legs follow, until I've got the backpack over my arm, and then I crab crawl down and sit next to River again.

One side of the sun slides out from behind a cloud. River's hair glistens with rain droplets, and I know mine will dry frizzy as an electrocuted cat. "Why don't you tell on Nancy?" I ask him.

"Usually my friends run interference," he says.

"What does that mean?"

"You know, the same as football. The players without the ball block so the ball carrier can run through the other team."

"Oh. Like Colin?"

"Yeah. And some fifth graders."

"But not me. And you told Miss Monaldo on me, didn't you?"

"Told her what?"

"That I was a bully bystander."

"No. Miss Monaldo asked me if you helped Nancy take my ball. I told her you didn't. That you're not like Nancy. And I told her you're the best dancer I've ever seen."

I don't know what to say. I don't deserve a friend like River. I think about the two best-friend girls in line for the tryouts. I think about Danita and Andrea. I make a decision.

"I have something to tell you. Actually two things. You did leave your phone in Danny's car. I put it in your backpack. And I read some of your poems and texts. And I'm sorry."

"You didn't." He twists his head to glare at me and clenches his fist.

"I'm sorry," I say again, giving him a crooked pleading smile.

He sighs and slides his hand along the bar. "Well, I'm sorry, too. Even though what I wrote was true, it probably didn't sound very nice, but I never broke my promise."

"True," I say. "You're not very good at being mean. I may have to give you lessons."

And River laughs because I'm funny. Then we both laugh.

"What's the other thing?" he asks.

"Papi called me. Because you made me put my phone number on the letters we sent. He got deported, and he's in a shelter across the border."

"Really? That's awesome," he says. "Well, not awesome about being deported. But awesome he called and he's okay."

"And Danny's going away for six weeks. And me and Danita got a bunk bed."

"Well that's highly illogical," River says. "Am I still your escort for the *quinceañera*? Danita didn't find a replacement for me, did she?"

I tap his arm and he stiffens. "Of course. If you want to." I reach into my back pocket and pull out a wet and falling-apart shamrock. I hand it to him. "It looked better before."

He studies it. Turns it sideways. Then upside down. "'Ucky friend. You. Not me,'" he reads.

I snatch the shamrock from him. Sure enough. The words melted and ran together from my wet pocket, and that's what it says: ucky friend. You. Not me.

"What a waste of fifty cents," I grumble. "It's supposed to say, 'I'm lucky I have a friend like you and not like me.'"

"It's the thought that counts. Of course, I'm not sure it makes sense to have a friend like yourself."

I hate it when River gets all know-it-all about things.

All of a sudden we hear an announcement coming from the outdoor speakers.

"Dinora Diaz. River Ramos-Henry. Please report to the office. DeeDee and River. Please report to the office."

"Oh. No," River says. "Help me down."

But hearing our names together over the speaker gives me an idea. "Hey, want to dance with me? For Spring Fling?"

I see a skeptical slant to River's eyes, behind his dripping hair.

"Not because I'm trying to make up for how stupid I acted."

"Then why?"

"Because I'm good. You're good. We're good together."

"You know some people will think it's a pity party, the Mexican diabetic and the deaf disabled kid."

"Then we better practice our bubblebutts off." I shoulder River's backpack and stay beside him, making sure his feet are steady on the rung below before he lets go with his hands. He heaves a big sigh once we're down. And so do I, but not because I'm off the jungle gym. I sigh because the cloud that covered my sun is gone. I link my arm in River's and we run through the last of the rain back inside.

We go straight to the office and explain what happened. When we finally get to class, the intercom buzzes.

"Yes?" says Mrs. Krewell.

"Would you please send Nancy to the office? She'll be leaving for the day."

River makes a weird face at me.

Yikes. What's going to happen to Nancy?

Samantha passes a note to Colin who passes it to Trevon who passes it to me. I slide it halfway into my desk and open it.

I'm sorry I was a bully bystander. I should have stuck up for you and River. Nancy is so jellus. (That's the way Samantha spelled jealous.) *She's afraid you'll steel her friends.* (Doesn't it seem like Samantha might need to go with me to reading group in Mr. Somerset's room, where we work on things like steal and steel?) I turn the note over and write, *It's okay. I was a bully bystander too. Nancy shouldn't be jealous.* I circle the word jealous. *I would never steal anything from her.* I circle the word steal, too.

River texts me after school.

I'm helping my mom with something. Over L8R?

Sure.

An hour later he knocks and walks in with a painting. Brilliant orange flowers with faces for their centers. Dancing flowers.

"I painted it after tryouts. You were the only one all the SLT members and fine arts teachers agreed on," he says.

A balloon starts to rise up from my heart. That doesn't sound like people felt sorry for me, or picked me for being Mexican or diabetic.

Danita struts out of her bedroom—I mean our bedroom—with Andrea. "Well, look who decided to visit. You have some catching up to do," she says to River.

"Nice to see you, too," says River.

For the next hour Danita puts on the playlist and I teach River the steps for the dances—the tricky *cumbia* steps and the moves for "*El Jarabe Tapatío.*" We're the same exact height, so it's easy for him to twirl me. And so he doesn't lose hold, I grab his hand in mine. I barely even notice his missing fingers.

Mami comes home with a grocery bag. She pulls out Mexican cokes and we take a break. She points to the painting. "Very nice," she says.

"I was surprised when I saw that orange dress," says River. "I thought you told me the dresses were Cerulean Blue."

Danita and Andrea fall over laughing.

Finally Danita chokes out, "They are blue. We don't wear dresses like that for *quinceañeras*."

Mami pats River then sits down. "*No te preocupes.* You still wear bull fighter costume for *quinceañera*."

We all laugh, except for River, not really sure what to believe.

"Don't worry," I tell him. "Mami's teasing. What are the guys wearing, Danita?"

"Just blue shirts, I think. Tuxedos and suits are so expensive."

"Just shirts?" says River, a little spark in his eyes. "No pants?"

Danita and Andrea jump up and pull him from the couch. Mami and I laugh.

River's phone goes off. "Make it so," he says. "Oh, no. I forgot. Let me ask."

He turns to Mami. "Is it okay if my mom brings dinner over?"

Mami sits up very straight. "You no need. We have food," say says in an unfriendly voice. I know she thinks it's charity and she hates charity more than Papi.

"No, it's not that. It's for a welcome. She didn't have a chance when you moved in."

The door opens and Danny walks in, followed by Mrs. Ramos-Henry. And she's carrying a glass pan with something that smells delicious, but different from anything I've smelled before.

Mami protests again, "No. No. You no need."

"No worries. We can argue about that another time," says Mrs. Ramos-Henry.

"What is it?" I blurt out.

"DeeDee, manners," says Mami.

"Chicken afritada," says River. "My favorite Filipino dinner."

Mrs. Ramos-Henry rushes the food to the kitchen, and Danita gets out plates and drinks.

River and I eat sitting at the puzzle table.

I spear a reddish hunk of something in among the potatoes, carrots, and chicken, and hold it up. "Is this a hot dog?"

"I know. Isn't it good?" He leans over and swipes it off my fork with his teeth, then gives me a hot dog grin. He whispers to me, "My mom and I did some research after school. She might have an idea about your dad."

Ah-ha. I thought it was a little fishy, welcoming us with dinner after we've been here over two months. "Really?" I ask.

I go back into the kitchen for seconds. I guess dancing and making up with your friend builds up your appetite. Mom and Mrs. Ramos-Henry are talking softly, eating at the little kitchen island. Danny leans on the counter, nodding and adding in some words when Mami doesn't understand. They're saying lawyer things, and I know they're talking about Papi.

Mami says, "DeeDee, listen."

Mrs. Ramos-Henry says, "I spoke to my friend this afternoon, and because your father is from a dangerous part of Mexico and you have diabetes, he may qualify for an extreme hardship six-oh-one waiver."

"At least I'm good for something," I say and they laugh.

I head back to River. "Do you know what they're talking about?" I ask River.

"My mom's friend works for the Immigrant Justice Center. Doctors for your diabetes will be better here than in Mexico, so she thinks there's a chance of proving your dad needs to be here to take care of you."

My stomach has that expanding feeling, from wanting to burst with emotions and maybe from eating too much chicken afritada. Here's my feelings. Papi alive—relieved. Papi maybe coming home—hopeful. Blabbing River's secret—guilty. River mad at me—sad. River my best friend—yippee! That's a lot of feelings on top of chicken afritada.

"Look, I found that piece we've been looking for." And River pushes a puzzle piece with a touch of Magenta into the missing spot.

"That's why we couldn't find it. It's not quite the same color." I compare the piece to the ones surrounding it.

"I think it's the shadow distorting it. Making it look different," says River.

Shadows do that, I think. Darken the colors. Like storm clouds. I gaze at my family. Danita and Andrea working on the *quinceañera* invites. Mami and Danny laughing at something Mrs. Ramos-Henry said. River and me searching for puzzle pieces. We're all normal, but not normal. The same in lots of ways, but different, too. The shadows change us, make us different colors, darken us, distort us. Me without friends. River without fingers. Danny without school. Mami without help. Danita without Papi. But even without Papi's light, when we're together, we brighten each other's shadows.

CHAPTER NINETEEN

D IS FOR AWESOME BECAUSE D IS FOR DEEDEE

River's not wearing anything special for Spring Fling, just an orange T-shirt that says ORANGE CRUSH under a picture of a stallion. He says it's a sports team but I've never heard of them. He has a red handkerchief, the same as real folkloric dancers. And we didn't tell anybody. Not even our families. It's a total surprise.

And if you're wondering, Nancy has in-school suspension and will miss almost all of the show, except when the fourth graders perform. Do I feel sorry for her? Maybe one quarter inch sorry. Because maybe she doesn't have a whole Starfleet of friends like I do— Dr. Ferreyra, Mrs. Marsh, Mrs. Krewell, Mami, Papi, Danita, Danny, Andrea, Mrs. Ramos-Henry, Yari, Nicole, Samantha, and most of all River.

It's a bright-as-a-penny day. I can't believe the SLT sold enough shamrocks to rent a big outdoor stage with the loudest speaker system in the world. Principal Sorry announced over the intercom for everyone to bring a plastic garbage bag and a towel in case the grass was wet or muddy. And all the classes get to sit and watch all Spring Fling afternoon. All afternoon. And do no work. What a glorious idea! I love Robert Frost Elementary.

I watch every act with my class until it's time to go change. On my way to get my dress I walk past a lady in a chair on the edge of the grass and recognize Mrs. Robinson.

"Nice to see you, DeeDee," she says. "What do you call a bear with no teeth?"

I'm so surprised I can't even think of an answer.

"A gummy bear." She laughs at her own joke and puts a clear bag tied with curly ribbons in my hand. A bag of sugar-free gummy bears. "Break a leg," she says.

"Thanks," I say and head to get my dress, wondering how she knew I gave her the shamrocks, and that I'm diabetic.

After I change I sneak around to stand behind the stage so nobody gets a preview of my mango-tango explosion dress. I'm nervous I'm not as good as everyone before me—the little first grade best-friend hip-hop dancers, the drummer who used two sticks in his hand and one in his mouth, the girl who belted out "Let It Go." I'm next. I cross my fingers and hope they pronounce my name right. Dee-Nor-uh. Dee-Nor-uh. Dee-Nor-uh.

"Please welcome DeeDee Diaz to the stage." Lucky for me, it's Yari's turn to do the announcing. She gives me a wave.

I walk up the steps to the microphone in slow motion, my stomach flip-flopping with flip-flops in it. A teacher comes over to adjust the height of the microphone. I stare at the audience.

I spy Mami sitting in a lawn chair next to River's mom. They're clapping outrageously and I haven't even danced yet. In front of them, Danny and Andrea and Danita sit on a blanket. Danny took off work. Danita and Andrea got an hour pass from their school. My family. I'm so full of love, and even though I miss Papi there's no room for sadness in my heart. I'm full of pepitas again.

I woke up a million times last night, and every time I practiced my intro speech until I fell back asleep. I open my mouth and wonder of wonders, my speech comes pouring out. "Hi everyone. My name is Dinora Diaz. My dance partner and I are going to dance a traditional Mexican folk dance from Jalisco, Mexico, where my parents first met each other. It's called '*El Jarabe Tapatio.*' I'd like to introduce my dance partner . . ."

River walks on stage and holds out the bandana to me.

Mami and Mrs. Ramos-Henry stand up.

I grab the end of the bandana and say, ". . . my best friend, River Ramos-Henry"

The music starts and we dance, shutting out everything—the audience, the stage, the screaming kids. I dance for Mami and Papi, who came here for a better life. I dance for Danny, the best brother in the world. I dance for Danita and Andrea, who taught me to dance and did my hair. And I dance for all the kids with distinctions, so they will know they can do it too. River's eyes dance as much as his feet do, and his hair whips around to the beat. I can't help smiling and smiling. From my mouth way down to my toes.

And then, too fast, it's over. River bows to me and then to the audience. I curtsy, swirling the skirt of my dress side to side one last time. Everyone is standing up. Some are clapping and chanting, "Encore, encore." Others are waving their arms in the air. I can't even see my family through the crowd.

Yari is waiting to announce the next act. She blows me a kiss. "*Bellisima*," she says as River and I pass her to go sit with our class.

After the fifth-grade acts I go change, but I almost don't want to. So many people stop and congratulate me, saying nice things—beautiful, amazing, spectacular, unique, dynamic. Only one person says, "I didn't know Mexicans could dance so well."

"Thanks," I say. "We all can't." Then I walk away fast.

Mrs. Marsh gives me a big hug when I stop for a quick check like she told me to. A little girl sits on the bench. "DeeDee, this is Jamiya," says Mrs. Marsh.

Jamiya waves at me in a shy way. "I have diabetes, too. Just like you," she says.

"She just moved here," says Mrs. Marsh, "and we were wondering if you'd be her peer tutor. Mrs. Krewell says you've made great progress."

"Peer tutor?" I don't know what to say.

"You're a really good dancer," says Jamiya.

"Thanks," I say. "Do you like to dance?"

"No," says Jamiya. "I love to dance."

When I finally push my way through the crowded hall, my best friend, River the celebrity, has a swarm of kids around him, including Yari and Colin.

"Hey," I say.

"Oh, DeeDee, you were great," says Yari. "I meant to ask you this morning, I'm having a slumber party for my birthday during spring break. Do you think your mom would let you come?"

River gives me a look. I know what he's thinking.

"Sure," I say, very casually. "But I don't play truth or dare."

"Oh, I hate those games. They're so mean." Yari makes a face. "Usually we go swimming or to the mall and then watch a movie. My mom's super strict." Then she heads toward a big group of fifth-grade girls.

I'm in shock. Me? She invited me to her sleepover. Can you believe it?

We walk to the front of the school to find our families, and Mami gives me a huge hug.

Danny puts one arm around my back and the other around River's shoulders. "You nailed it, bro," he says to River. "Keep practicing. I'll be back for Danita's *quinceañera* and you're my wingman."

River turns to Colin and says, "Hey Colin, this is Danny, my big brother wannabe."

Mami beams at all of us. "Banana Split?" she asks. "To celebrate?"

"I love that place," says Colin.

"Come with. My mom can drop you off after," says River.

"Beam me up, Scotty," says Colin, and River gives him the Star Trek salute.

I give River a look. And a little smile. Always keep your door open for a true friend, I think. And open it wide enough for their friend, too.

Cars jam the parking lot and teachers with orange vests dash around waving their arms. Where is Danny's car? We might never make it to Banana Split. I see Nancy leaning against the front of a minivan parked in a disabled parking spot. Well, la-di-da, I think. Look who's breaking the law to get a primo parking spot for Spring Fling. But then I notice Nancy's mom is lifting a little boy out of a wheelchair and into the back seat.

"I'll be right back," I tell Danny and walk over to Nancy's van.

"Hello, DeeDee," says Mrs. Wang. "It's nice to see you again. I enjoyed your performance. This is Nancy's kindergarten brother, Austin."

"Nice to meet you," I say, but Austin doesn't say anything back. He gazes past me, asleep with his eyes open. Mrs. Wang wipes a little dribble from his lips, lifts his legs, and pivots him into the car. Then she starts to collapse the wheelchair. A sticker on the back window of the van says, I'M THE PROUD PARENT OF A NORTHLAKE VALEDICTORIAN.

"I didn't know you had a little brother," I say to Nancy. "I didn't see him at the sleepover."

Nancy has been crying. I'm sure of it. Her eyes are red and her nose is swollen. She stares at the ground and mutters, "Austin stays with my dad every other weekend to give my mom a break. He needs a lot of attention. My other brother is away at college."

As more kids stream down the sidewalk, Nancy slides lower and lower until she's sitting on the fender of the van.

I go around the side door and smile at Austin. He nods his head at me and makes a sound. Nancy's mom reaches in and buckles his seatbelt. "Why does Austin need a wheelchair?" I ask Mrs. Wang. Some people, Mami for one, would tell me to mind my manners, but I'm not afraid of disabilities.

"Cerebral palsy," she says. "Nancy's a little shy about being in public with Austin, but he loves Spring Fling."

I can't believe what a selfish brat Nancy is. Being embarrassed about her own brother. Just because he's in a wheelchair. As if disabilities are the plague.

I'm about to walk back and wait for Danny to bring the car when I stop myself. Nancy is no different from me. I was embarrassed about being friends with River in public. I treated him horribly, pretended I didn't know him. I even denied being his friend. But I was lucky enough to get a wake-up call from River's Padlet, and from Danny and Papi. And just in time to be able to dance with my best friend and show off my Mexican heritage, and represent people with distinctions.

I walk back to the front of the van. Mrs. Wang stands talking to another mom. What did River write in his Padlet? *People don't deserve second and third chances until they learn from their mistakes*. Well, how do you know if someone has learned from their mistakes unless you give them a second chance?

"I think your little brother is cute," I say to Nancy. "River would say he's got distinction. And my brother is going away, too, like your brother at college. He's in the National Guard."

Nancy lifts her eyes to my face. She squints and scrutinizes me. "You don't have to be nice to me. I don't deserve it."

"You're not the only one who does mean things," I say.

"I don't know," she says. "At first I didn't really think I was a bully, but Dr. Souriyavongsa made me write down everything mean I've done and compare my list with what the teachers said."

"Holy jalapeño, that stinks," I say. For the first time, Nancy doesn't sound stuck-up and bossy. She sounds scared.

"DeeDee, I'm so sorry for everything I did. I really am," she says with a little snuffle. "And I didn't mean it about Spring Fling. You're a really good dancer."

"River was an amazing partner," I say.

Nancy lets out a sigh. "And I'm sorry about River, too. He sticks up for his friends. You're lucky. I'm such a baby for getting jealous just because I wanted attention. I don't know what my problem is."

"I have an idea. Next year we'll all try out together so we'll all get attention." I feel about as big as the school. My heart is light and feathery.

"Are you kidding? River won't ever speak to me again after what I did to him."

"Then we'll dare him to do it, and that's the truth," I say, hoping she puts two and two together and comes up with sleepover.

She does and says, "That was a disaster. Did you know Samantha called her mom to pick her up, too? And I got grounded. River is never going to forgive me for that."

Is it bad if I'm secretly happy she called the sleepover a disaster and got grounded? That's one way to learn from your mistakes, isn't it?

"River is the master of second chances," I say. "You don't live long and prosper unless you let people learn from their mistakes." I copy River's salute when I say this.

"Nancy," Mrs. Wang calls. "We've got to go. Austin is getting tired."

Nancy straightens up and walks around to the side of the van.

"We're all going to Banana Split, if you want to come," I say, hoping it's not too soon for River to be ready with a second chance. "It's a place in my old neighborhood."

Nancy glances over at the group waiting for me and shakes her head.

Mrs. Wang asks, "Is it next to a park? I was there a long time ago."

"You can follow us, if you want."

"We'd love that, wouldn't we, Nancy?" Mrs. Wang gets in the car.

Nancy doesn't answer.

I put my hand on her arm and lean close to her. "Don't you wonder what kind of ice cream bubblebutts eat?"

Nancy lets out a little snort—a tiny bit of a giggle. "You're my funniest friend," she says and opens her car door. She smiles at me. "Don't you wonder if they serve noodles to noodlenoses at Banana Split?"

"Look who's funny," I say. And we both laugh. A gut-busting, new-beginning, pepita-planting laugh.

ACKNOWLEDGMENTS

"Give me your tired, your poor,
Your huddled masses yearning to breathe free,
The wretched refuse of your teeming shore.
Send these, the homeless, tempest-tost to me,
I lift my lamp beside the golden door!"
—Emma Lazarus

The Statue of Liberty stands in New York City—a symbol of more than a century of weaving immigrants into the fabric of our "perfect Union" where together we establish Justice, insure domestic Tranquility, provide for the Common Defense, promote the general Welfare, and secure the Blessings of Liberty to ourselves and our Posterity. We are a nation of immigrants.

But where is the lamp beside the golden door today? In 2017 ICE removed 226,119 undocumented immigrants. Forty-three percent were non-criminals.

Over seventy six percent of American adults believe that immigrants strengthen our country and over fifty percent of American adults believe that undocumented immigrants should be allowed to pursue citizenship.

Writing Another D for DeeDee forced me to think about the collateral damage being caused when families are split apart and how children's lives hang in the balance. The basic human rights of life, liberty and the pursuit of happiness shouldn't be attainable only if born as a United States citizen. Between 1892 and 1954 over twelve million immigrants arrived at Ellis Island, pursuing the American Dream in a country designed to protect the human spirit. TWELVE MILLION. Yet in 2017, we're turning away over 310,000 immigrants at the southern border of our country, and 41,500 are children.

I understand that we want a safe and stable country. I understand that some immigrants enter the United States to perpetrate gang activity and peddle drugs. Of course we want to protect our country. I also understand that criteria need to be met before immigrants attain legal status. But what if the twelve million immigrants arriving at Ellis Island had to wait five years before even applying to become a United States citizen? What if it cost $800 for a green card to become a resident, and then $900 to become a citizen?

I am the granddaughter of immigrants. Both sets of my grandparents were born in other countries. And my life is enriched by the many immigrants I call friends. I'm not a gifted politician or lawyer, but those who are must be able to figure out a way to welcome "the tired, the poor, the huddled masses yearning to breathe free." And a way to simplify the process of becoming a naturalized United States citizen.

It is always my goal to write books that represent the students I've been privileged to teach, but writing outside of my own cultural background requires help from so many people. I'm humbled by the willingness of authenticity readers to sift through my manuscript for inaccuracies and misrepresentations. And so I have a long list of people to thank:

First and most importantly, Daisy Olveras, a former East Aurora District 131 Allen Elementary School student, who loved my first book Canned and Crushed, but kept bugging me to write a book about a girl. Daisy allowed me to accompany her on her visits to monitor her diabetes while I was writing Another D for DeeDee. As a first grader, Ashley Mack, another Allen Elementary School student with diabetes, participated in a first grade enrichment group and as a treat for completing assignments I passed out jelly beans, not aware that she had diabetes. Even good teachers make mistakes and need to be educated. Thanks to both Daisy and Ashley for educating me and making me a better teacher and writer.

I met Yeris Mayol-Garcia on the train to South Bend in 2016. She commented on the book I was reading, The Distance Between Us by Reyna Grande and we began a conversation. What a coincidence that Yeris had just completed a Ph.D. graduate study program at Penn State and had accepted a coveted position at the U.S. Census Bureau in Washington D.C. Yeris' research focuses on how parental migration affects children and her input on Another D for DeeDee was invaluable.

Jeanne McDonald and Marsha Evitts worked alongside me for many years in East Aurora, District 131. Jeanne teaches hard of hearing students and Marsha supports students as a school nurse. Jeanne helped me get my facts straight about students who are hard of hearing and Marsha instructed me on diabetic care for students. Having both of these resources at my fingertips was a phenomenal advantage. And then, as if I wasn't enough of a bother, they both agreed to read my rough draft and give me feedback.

Josiah VanWingerden, a senior at Whitworth University in Spokane, WA, advocates for students with disabilities. He says, "I am certainly not the 'typical' Whitworth student, for instance, I am part of a minority race, use a wheelchair to get around, and am adopted. In these ways, I am the non-normative student. I want to be an educator and advocator so that I can validate each person's experience. This is what inspired me to become a student-leader." This amazing college student gave me unbelievable feedback for Another D for DeeDee as I struggled to get it right when portraying a character with disabilities.

Kyle Jacobson, copy editor for Madison Essentials Magazine, and passionate skater coached me on skateboard lingo, for which DeeDee, River and skaters who read will forever be thankful.

The current #ownvoices makes me determined to find authentic voices and include them in my story. Even though I've worked with marginalized students my entire teaching career, I can't presume to understand how it feels or appropriate the specific culture correctly without advice from authentic voices. Third grade teacher, Ada Carrillo, and Allen Elementary administrative assistant, Sonia Fonseca, patiently helped me avoid using words from my Spanish dictionary that made no sense. Doctoral student Judith Legoretta and East Aurora District 131 Johnson Elementary School principal Dr. Rita Guzman, supplied much needed specifics about undocumented status, deportation, and *quinceañeras. Gracias. Dios las bendigas.*

Editors hold a special place in my heart for taking shapeless blobs of stories and molding them into beautiful books. Thank you to Rachel Stark and Kirsten Kim, who worked tirelessly on my messy blob.

As always, my husband and family fuel my emotional well-being—you know who you are—with a special shout-out to brand-new Ruby Lynn Lipsker, born February 10, 2018—a baby in my arms while revising my manuscript. My writing sisters motivate me to keep writing—Christine DeSmet, Cheryl Hanson, Julie Holmes, Blair Hull, Lisa Kusko, Martha Miles, and Roi Solberg.

And the words of my God convict me—Jeremiah 22:3 "Do justice and righteousness, and deliver the one who has been robbed from the power of his oppressor. Also do not mistreat or do violence to the foreigner, the orphan, or the widow."